James Boylan's stories have appeared in numerous literary magazines, including *Quarterly West, Confrontation,* and *Florida Review.* This is his first book.

DISCARD

REMIND ME TO MURDER YOU LATER

JOHNS HOPKINS: POETRY AND FICTION
John T. Irwin, General Editor

Remind Me
to Murder You Later

Short Stories by
JAMES BOYLAN

THE JOHNS HOPKINS UNIVERSITY PRESS
BALTIMORE AND LONDON

This book has been brought to publication with the generous assistance of the G. Harry Pouder Fund.

© 1988 The Johns Hopkins University Press
All rights reserved
Printed in the United States of America

The Johns Hopkins University Press
701 West 40th Street   Baltimore, Maryland 21211
The Johns Hopkins Press Ltd., London

LIBRARY OF CONGRESS CATALOGING-IN-PUBLICATION DATA

Boylan, James, 1958–
  Remind me to murder you later.
  (Johns Hopkins, poetry and fiction)
  I. Title. II. Series.
PS3552.0914R46   1988   813′.54   88-45417
ISBN 0-8018-3728-6 (alk. paper)

The writing of these stories was made possible in part by a grant from the Pennsylvania State Council on the Arts.

Some stories in this volume first appeared, in somewhat different form, in the following periodicals, to whose editors grateful acknowledgment is made: *American Bystander:* "Dictionary Art Review"; *Confrontation:* "Bride of Frankenstein"; *Florida Review:* "Fugue for Violin and Three Stooges" and "Invisible Woman"; *Quarterly West:* "Thirty-six Miracles of Lyndon Johnson" and "Jimmy Durante Lost in Antarctica"; and *Western Humanities Review:* "Potter's Field." "Dictionary Art Review" was reprinted in *Writer's Digest.*

for Deirdre

✦ Contents

REMIND ME TO MURDER YOU LATER

✦ Bride of Frankenstein

Exactly three days before her wedding, Rachel Ilanovitch drank an unexpected quantity of light green ink. Ink, incapable of ending her life, was successful in staining her veins and arteries a shade of dark ocher, so that Rachel Ilanovitch came to resemble a stalk of celery left too long in a glass of colored water. Kate Hampton, the maid of honor, drove to Rachel's house on Ash Wednesday, the day the wedding was to have taken place, bringing with her a package of heavy pancake make-up wrapped in a green ribbon. Kate was considerate and did not want her friend to be embarrassed by the relentlessness of her all-too-visible circulation.

Kate was a reporter for the *Evening Sentinel* in Valley Forge. The last story she had done before taking time off for Rachel's wedding concerned a dairy farmer who had been struck by a two-foot-long icicle. The farmer's widow kept referring to her husband in the present tense, and pointed out the window toward the barn, where a pair of milk pails lay on their sides in the snow.

Kate stopped her car next to a snowbank and looked up the hill toward the Ilanovitches' stone farmhouse.

On the dashboard of Kate's car was a book of poems. She was supposed to have read one aloud as part of the homily. Something by Emily Dickinson. She had marked her place in the volume with a queen from a pack of playing cards.

Kate checked her appearance in the rear-view mirror, nervous. Leaving the book of poems behind, she struggled through the ice toward the stone slabs of the Ilanovitches' porch. No footsteps had disturbed the snow. From a second-story window a drape opened, disclosed a face, fell dark again. In her coat pocket, Kate's fingers felt the shells of roasted peanuts.

Kate pulled on the brass knocker, waited, leaned into the house and called. There was no answer. She unbuttoned her long coat in the hallway, squinted upward toward a staircase. "Hello?"

The Ilanovitches had a Dalmatian named Vanya. Kate inched around the front hall and the cluttered parlor, waiting to be growled at. She had

been to the Ilanovitches' many times as a child, less since the death of
Rachel's father. On the piano were a dozen framed photographs of
Rachel, her mother, her father, others. A crystal bowl of wrapped candy
stood next to a bouquet of dried flowers. Above a fireplace was an oil
painting of some hunters shooting Canadian geese.

"Hello?"

Kate hung her coat on the newel and slid her fingertips along the
banister. All the shades in the house seemed to be down; as she looked
upward into the darkness of the spiraling stairs she had the impression
that she was looking into a whirlpool. She placed a hand at the bottom of
her throat.

From a distant room came a soft scraping sound, like the sound of
someone shoveling snow. Kate stepped forward. An empty bottle of
champagne stood on a deep windowsill. Next to it, two glasses. One of the
glasses was half-full; the other lay on its side. She pulled back a curtain,
looked out on the fields: stalks of dead corn poked through the snow. To
the north was the house of Rachel's fiancé, Victor. Vic's family had a
springhouse that stood, ice-bound, on the edge of a creek that ran onto
the Ilanovitches' land. A scarecrow stood arms-open next to the frozen
stream. Icicles hung from its hands.

There were two rooms on the second floor. The scraping sound came
from a guest room, its door closed. The door was unpainted; the wood
was scarred by dents and cuts. Some marks were clearly the results of
Vanya's claws.

Across the hall, Rachel's mother's room was dark. A brass fan covered
an unused fireplace.

"Hello?" Kate said.

The scraping stopped.

"Who's there?"

"Kate Hampton," Kate said. "It's me."

Kate opened the door. She smelled warm glue and soap.

Rachel's mother stood in overalls in the middle of the room, one hand
holding a straight razor. Parts of the walls were damp, turning the party
hats and confetti on the wallpaper dark. In other portions of the room,
the paper was missing altogether; it lay in long strips upon the bare floor.

"Oh," Rachel's mother said. "It's you then."

"What are you doing?"

"Scraping," said Mrs. Ilanovitch. She pointed with the razor.
"Look."

She motioned to a section of the wall where the wallpaper had been stripped. There, in flowing green script, were the words "February 12, 1872. Elizabeth Amis Harkness." Beneath these words was a series of ink blots.

Mrs. Ilanovitch, covered with paste, looked at Kate suspiciously. "What *is* that on your forehead, honey?" she said.

"Ashes," said Kate. "It's Ash Wednesday."

"Oh. I didn't know. Makes you look Indian or something."

"Who is that?"

"Who is who?"

"The woman who signed the wall."

"Oh, her. One of the Harknesses. They built this place. There's more over there. A love poem. This must have been her room."

Kate stepped through the scraps to read the wall.

"Don't bother," Mrs. Ilanovitch said. "It's garbage." She looked at Kate curiously again. "How come they put that stuff on your forehead?" she said.

Kate shrugged politely. "It's for penitence."

"Penitence?"

"Yes."

"Well, if you say so. I don't know. I say it makes you look Indian."

"It's not supposed to."

"Well," Mrs. Ilanovitch said. "It does." She turned to the wall again and started scraping. "Go on upstairs. Rachel's waiting for you."

Kate shut the door. The sun shone through the window on the landing, casting light on the hardwood floors.

She found Rachel lying stomach-down in her bed, wearing only a lace bra and reading a thick book. The bridal gown hung on a hook next to a small writing desk.

"Hello, Katie," Rachel said.

"Hello, Rache." Kate sat down on the bed and put her arm on Rachel's shoulderblades. The veins in Rachel's back fanned out like green highways. Kate traced them with one finger.

"What are you doing?"

"Reading." Rachel dropped her head into the book. "That feels good," she said. "It feels better when you touch them. My veins, I mean. They itch."

"What are you reading?"

"Frankenstein."

She showed Kate the book: a leather-bound volume with gilt edges and dark green endpapers.

"I've never read it before," Rachel said. "So different from the movie. So sad."

"I saw Vic," Kate said.

"They wind up at the North Pole," Rachel said. "He chases the monster across the frozen waste."

"He said for me to send you his love."

Rachel looked out the window, her eyelids blinking in half-panic. "He's a bastard," she said.

Rachel rolled over onto her back, breathing heavily. Green veins ran up the sides of her neck; a network of blackish threads spread outward from her breast.

Kate rested her palm on her friend's temples, blotting her tears with the edge of her thumb. "Why'd you do it, Rachel?" she said. "The ink, I mean."

"What do you care?"

"I care." Kate rubbed Rachel's forehead. "Really, I care."

"I told Victor," Rachel said. "He didn't understand."

"I'll understand."

Rachel paused.

"I wanted to show him what I'm capable of," she said.

From downstairs, Kate heard the scraping of Rachel's mother's razor.

"You wanted to show him you were capable—of what?"

The house creaked. There was the sound of something sliding on the roof above them. There was silence, then a distant shattering; a sheet of ice had melted off the shingles and crashed on the stone porch below.

"He's seeing someone," Rachel said. "I know it. I'm not stupid."

"He's seeing someone? How do you know?"

"I know."

"Have you talked this over with him?"

"I did. When he came. He said I was crazy. He sat on my desk and said I was crazy." She pointed to her little desk. There were shells of roasted peanuts on the floor.

"I brought you this," Kate said. She handed Rachel the box with the green ribbon. "A wedding present."

"You mean a staying-single present," Rachel said. She pointed to the desk. "Put it over there. Next to my books."

"Don't you want to see what it is?"

"I don't know. What is it?"

"It's make-up. To cover up your veins."

Rachel looked confused. "But I want them to show. I wouldn't have done it if I didn't want them to show."

Downstairs the sound of scraping ceased.

"Your dress is pretty," Kate said.

"Yours is in the closet."

"I still have to pay you for it."

"Save your money, Kate. We're returning them."

"Are you sure?" Kate said. "Don't you want to wait and see what happens?"

Rachel looked toward her books. One of her fingers fell on her throat and traced her green jugular down the side of her neck.

"I know what's going to happen," she said.

They sat in silence for a while.

"Will you do me a favor?" Rachel asked.

"Of course. All you have to do is ask."

"I want you to put on your bridesmaid's dress. The one we made for you. And then I want you to read me the poem you were going to read at the wedding. Just so it's not a total loss. I love the way you read. You have a nice voice. It's very realistic."

Kate swallowed. "I don't know, Rache. Pretty weird."

Rachel looked away. "I knew you wouldn't do it."

"I didn't say I wouldn't do it," Kate said. She stood. "I said it was weird. I didn't say I wouldn't do it."

"Thank you, Kate. You're a real friend."

"Where's the dress?"

"In the closet. You'll see them all hanging in a row. Your name is on yours."

Kate opened the closet. The bridesmaids' dresses hung in plastic bags.

"Rachel . . . " Kate said. "They're black."

"I know."

"They were white when we had them fitted," Kate said, peeling back the plastic.

"We dyed them."

Rachel reached for *Frankenstein*.

"See, with everyone in white it wasn't clear who the bride was."

Kate ran her fingers along the black fabric. "You're sure about this?"

"Do it for me."

"I'll have to get the poems. The book's in the car."

"Take your time," Rachel said. "Here. Don't forget the shoes."

"Okay. Stay right here. I'll be back."

"I'm not going anywhere."

Kate put the dress on in the hallway and squinted at herself in a mirror. The dye had not stained the fabric evenly; it oscillated across the lace in shades of gray, blackish-gray, and blue.

Kate stood in the hallway, looking at herself. Rachel turned a page in her book.

The stairs creaked beneath Kate's heels as she went down to the second floor. The sun had vanished from the wood floors. Mrs. Ilanovitch's door was closed.

In the guest room the wallpaper lay in great heaps upon the floor. Kate stepped over the shards and squinted at the bare plaster.

"You really have no shame, have you?" Rachel's mother said, standing in the doorway.

"Mrs. Ilanovitch?"

"Look at you. You know what you look like in that getup?"

"But Rachel asked me—."

"It's you, isn't it?" Mrs. Ilanovitch said.

"Excuse me?"

"It's you. You and Victor. Isn't it?"

Kate stood in the ruined room, rustling.

"I was reading that poem," Mrs. Ilanovitch said. "The one the Harkness girl wrote. Under the wallpaper. It suddenly occurred to me it was you."

"I'm sorry," Kate said.

"You aren't sorry," Rachel's mother said. "You don't have a drop of shame in your body."

"I've got shame," Rachel said. She thought of the milk pails on their sides in the snow. "You don't know."

"Don't tell me what I know. I've got you all sized up."

"Do you want me to leave, Mrs. Ilanovitch?"

"I think that would be a good start."

Mrs. Ilanovitch held up the razor. "Here," she said. "You'll want this. As a little memento."

Kate walked out of the room into the dark house. "I don't want any mementos," she said.

She walked back downstairs, past the dark parlor with the old piano and the crystal bowl of wrapped candy. She picked her coat up off the newel, braced herself for the cold.

She closed the front door and slowly walked across the stone porch. The ice that had fallen off the roof earlier now lay in broken crystals. A window opened overhead; the straight razor sailed through the air and into the snow.

An icicle fell off of the springhouse roof. There was the sound of something moving through snow, an animal snarling.

Vanya walked around the far side of Kate's car. He showed her his teeth. Vanya's breath vaporized around his nostrils.

Kate stopped, stepped backward, snow brushing her ankles. Vanya stepped forward, growling. Kate stepped back again, slipped on the ice. Her hands pushed into the wet snow. Vanya looked at her, curious. The razor lay on the ice near her elbow.

She grasped the razor and stood. The back of her black dress was covered with white snow.

Kate held out the razor, shaking it at the dog. Vanya growled. He stood in her path. It was not possible to walk toward the car. Kate could see the book of poems lying on the dashboard, the queen of spades sticking out of the gilt-edged pages.

Kate took a step backward into the snow, keeping an eye on Vanya. The sun was sinking now, and the lights in Victor's house, two miles distant, were gray and dim.

Holding her weapon, Kate stepped north, inching her way backward across the frozen waste.

✦ Fugue for Violin and Three Stooges

All night long Moe has been reading a story about a spider and a pig, until at last, toward dawn, he sighs and tips over backward in his Kennedy rocker. Everything is blurred and dark in Moe's eyes: the sun rising through winter branches is transformed into the dark veins on Carla's throat. He is almost blind. There is a mirror above the Ebenezer Scrooge fireplace, in which Moe sees himself horizontal. He says: "Remind me to murder you later."

Larry lies awake in the hospital, thinking of titles for his autobiography. A nurse checks the tubes in Larry's nose. Moe already used *I Stooge to Conquer*. For a while Larry leaned toward *Porcupine: A Life*, but now he prefers *You Bastard Moe*. Everything is blurred and dark in Larry's memory: the sun is rising through the willows as Carla's mother gives birth in a Columbia pictures warehouse filled with props and Wild West scenery. He is almost blind. His face is reflected ovoid in a jewel on the nurse's throat. "I can't see," he says. "I can't see." She gets the doctor. "He can't see," she says. "What's wrong, Mr. Fine?" "I've got my eyes closed," Larry says.

Carla puts on her make-up, checks her hair in the rear-view mirror en route to her job at Schnederwitz, Beowolf and Chang. She is almost blonde. Everything is blurred and dark because the Xerox machine is malfunctioning. "It needs more toner," she says. In the evening young Ratt is proposing. They drink wine until it's early then spend the morning on her fold-out sofa bed as a television turns their faces blue and gray.

Moe is watching the birds. He has a feeder outside the window. He's wearing the Liberace bathrobe now. There are two loons from the swamp that have laid their eggs in the nest of a mourning dove. The doves are raising the loons. Moe is about to finish *Charlotte's Web*. She's almost dead. Moe puts the book down on the mantel in front of the mirror to rest his eyes. He's reading *Charlotte's Web*. Moe likes the author's initials, and says them out loud. "E. B.," Moe says. The loons peck at their parents. "Eee bee bee bee bee bee bee."

Larry is watching the Cardinals. He's got a new name for his book: *I'm Going to Kill You Moe You Stupid-Ass Son of a Bitch*. When Larry was young he played one season for the Philadelphia Athletics. He chipped a bone in his foot and had to leave the team. For a time he was a professional violinist. He changed his name from Fineberg to Fine the week before Warren Harding ate poisoned fish. While performing at the Trocodero on Arch Street he met Moe Howard and his little brothers, Shemp and Curly. These days the Troc is a Chinese theater showing pornographic movies. "Time for your bath, Mr. Fine," the nurse says, as the batter swings and misses. "I'll come when I'm ready," Larry says. Three and two the count. The nurse is playing with the jewel on her necklace. "Are you ready?" A swing and the batter's retired. "I'm ready."

Carla and her lover are watching *The Birds*. Her heart is pulsing into the palm of his hand. His fingers stroke a necklace with tiny silver links which is coiling loosely on her left nipple. There are two tiny masks on the chain: comedy and tragedy. "Which do you want?" says Ratt. Nickety nackety now now now. "A Conservative rabbi," she says. "From the synagogue in my hometown." "I didn't know you were Jewish," he says. The nipple puckers like a suction cup. "Howard isn't a Jewish name." Nickety nackety hey Johnny rackety now now now. "They changed it from Horowitz." All the crows are on the jungle gym now. "I don't mind. It's just that my mother will insist on a minister. I mean, there it is. She likes to get her own way." Riselty raselty nickety nackety hey Johnny rackety now now now.

Moe is eating a banana when he sees the mailman coming down the street. He drops the peel, puts on his cashmere coat, meets him at the box. "Afternoon, Mr. Howard." There is another big check from Columbia pictures. "Why don't you get a hair cut?" Moe says to the postman. The postman gives Moe the peace sign. "Peace," he says. Moe makes the peace sign. The two of them are both making peace signs. Moe jabs his fingers forward and pokes his peace fingers in the postman's eyes. "Son of a bitch!" the postman yells. "Of all the stupid, pitiful—." Moe says: "Nyk nyk nyk."

Larry is having his afternoon nap when the mail comes. The nurse leaves the Blue Cross bills on the dresser, next to the photograph of Carla. The door clicks softly behind her. Larry opens his eyes. Light is streaming through the willows, and Curly and Shemp are standing there. Moe gave them both strokes. Curly's real name was Jerome. Moe's real name was Moses. They all have heart trouble. A bearded Moses is standing behind Curly and Shemp holding a tablet. "Oh," Curly says. "A wise guy."

Carla's lover is lying face down upon her. His chest is resting between her legs. She can feel his heart beating. "You give good heart," she says. He pulls himself up and kisses the masks. "When did your father die?" "Twenty-five years ago," she says. "Christmas Eve." Angela Cartwright is upset because they're leaving the lovebirds in the house. "Do you have any other family? I mean living?" "My half-uncle," she says. "He's Fine."

Moe loves the music. Hello, hello, hello. Hello! They're showing "A Plumbing We Will Go." One of Curly's. Water fills up the clockface, and the black cook says, "This house sho gone crazy." There's a sound like water moving through the strings of a harpsichord. Niagara Falls! Slowly I turned.... Larry disappears in a hole he's been digging in the front yard of the rich people. Step by step! Inch by inch! The phone rings. It has the sound of bad news. Moe lets it ring until the commercial, then gets up, slips on the banana peel, falls forward into the mantel, dislodges the mirror. Seven years bad luck. Moe looks at a jagged reflection. The phone stops. "Remind me to murder you later," he says.

When the nurse comes in, the corpse is cold and "A Plumbing We Will Go" is on the television with the sound off. Larry, Shemp, and Curly are in a little boat surrounded by cherubs. "Hey, Larry," Shemp says. "Play your violin." "Yeah," says Curly. "You never play your violin anymore." "Yeah," says Shemp. "You never do. What's the big idea?" A wave picks them up. The sound of "Listen to the Mockingbird" disappears in salt.

Carla and her lover are falling asleep in each other's arms. The dark is broken: Hello, hello, hello. Hello! It's "A Plumbing We Will Go." Carla wakes up, looks around the dark room for her shirt. The veins on her throat are darkening. Ratt shrinks from her.

"Oh God," he says. "Mother hates these guys." He squints. "So do I."

Carla shivers. Slowly she turns. Step by step. Inch by inch. Niagara Falls!

"Me three," she says.

✦ Horse Year

Brian was walking a bluetick hound toward the covered bridge where Mr. Bowman, the sixth-grade teacher, had hanged himself on Earth Day. The only light came from Brian's house, a quarter mile behind. A lamp was on in Koren's room. She was probably still crying. It had sounded like she was going to be crying for a long time.

Brian's mother had come through the door five minutes earlier, her eyes red, holding his sister the way one would hold a fragile thing, as if Koren were a candle about to go out. They wouldn't tell him what had happened. His mother just told him to get out and walk the dog and that was it. He got Alex and went out into the night although this was the hour when there were things that could get you. There was a kind of groaning in the trees as wind moved through the dark pines and hemlock. Alex, a coon dog, pulled Brian toward the covered bridge, where it was reasonably certain Mr. Bowman's ghost waited for him. In school Mr. Bowman had been a sad and exhausted man, looking like a slave on some sort of Roman warship. The week before his death, he had taught the class about plants that ate insects, dinosaurs that ate plants, and certain monks in Tibet who ate nothing, but sat cross-legged throughout the day in cool stone caves concentrating on their respiration.

These breathatarians, according to Mr. Bowman, were sometimes able to make themselves rise off the floor and float. When he said this, Mr. Bowman had looked even sadder and more worn out than usual. Someone had asked Mr. Bowman if he wanted to be a breathatarian, but he did not answer. He looked out the window, sighed, then gave a surprise quiz. The quiz, for some reason, consisted of only answers, to which the class had to try to guess the questions. One of the "answers" was "flax," the chief export of Argentina; another was "thirty-two." Mr. Bowman had hanged himself before grading the quizzes, so no one ever knew what "thirty-two" was the answer to. Jimmy Holtzman said that "thirty-two" was how many years it took the light from Alpha Centauri, the nearest star, to reach the earth, but someone else said that "thirty-two" was how old Mr. Bowman would be if on Earth Day he hadn't hanged himself. Sean Tubman said he waited until Earth Day to make some sort of statement, but what the statement was no one could guess, unless it had something to do with the importance of ecology.

✦　✦　✦

Koren cried in her room upstairs. In the kitchen, Mrs. Keleher sat at the kitchen table drinking Jameson's Irish whiskey. She looked through a small telephone book, trying to find the current number of Koren's father. She picked up the phone and began to dial. Upstairs, Koren wailed in disbelief, amazed and shipwrecked in her purple bedroom.

✦　✦　✦

The parents of Brian's dog were two foxhounds from the stable, Penny and Gomer. Gomer didn't hunt much. Mostly he sat on Mr. Kingman's front porch asleep, occasionally lifting his head to snap at moths and dragonflies. Mr. Kingman was a large, red-haired tobacco-chewing Democrat. He gave the Kelehers a deal on stable space in exchange for Koren breaking in the ponies. Before the divorce Mr. and Mrs. Keleher also used to ride, but that was in order to be included as members of the Strafford Hunt Club. Koren's mother was still a member of the Hunt but no longer attended the luncheons. The old clubhouse was dowdy and strange, as if inhabited by a cotillion of upper-crust apparitions.

✦　✦　✦

Kingman's stables held twenty-two ponies and sixteen horses, most of which were tired and resentful slave-beasts. The stalls had once been painted white but were now mostly mud and beige. Mice that lived in the barn sometimes turned up in the stone water bowls built into the walls. There were snakes, too, which Kingman's weird son, Dudley, captured and kept in a broken aquarium. Sometimes the girls would find Dudley trapping mice in their ponies' stalls. Later, they said, he forced his snakes to eat them.

　　Koren's first show had been Ludwig's Corners. Her father had sat in a lawn chair all day, watching the entrants in the baby green class, making notes on a clipboard he had borrowed from the office. Koren had taken fourth in the novice jumper class for small ponies. They took a photograph. Koren fed Jester a carrot as the white ribbon hung from the bridle. In the background, Brian stood holding a cup of instant hot chocolate he had bought from the Weenie-wagon. The Weenie man had poured the powder into a styrofoam cup, then added boiling hot water and stirred this all around with a stick. On top there was foam.

✦ ✦ ✦

Koren and Brady lay on their backs, blowing smoke rings in a kind of island in a swamp. The rings traveled straight up in the air, revolving. Jester and Iris chewed moss at the base of willow tree, as muck from the swamp dried on their hocks and gaskins.

"We have to get back soon," Brady said, rolling onto her stomach. "Or we'll never get back."

"So we never get back," Koren said, still staring into the sky. She blew another ring. "Like who will notice."

Brady blew a long line of gray smoke out in front of her.

"Kingman will notice."

"He won't. No one notices anything."

Brady pushed back her hair.

"I have to get back," she said. "I have to braid for the show tomorrow."

"What you have to start now?"

"I have to wash Iris so I can start braiding. It's going to take me like ten thousand years anyway. It's got to be perfect."

"Why don't you get Wisty to do it?"

"Wisty did it last time and the whole thing came undone. I mean like I had to stay up till like four in the morning redoing it."

Somewhere in the distance a car started honking.

Brady stubbed out her cigarette. "I have to get back."

"Has Wisty ever been here?" Koren said. "With you, Brady?"

"No. This is the first time I ever brought anyone."

"Let's like, not tell her or anything," Koren said. "Okay?"

"Okay."

Koren leaned forward. "Let's not tell Nicole, either," she whispered.

"All right. We won't."

Koren inhaled, trying to smell her own mouth. "Hey, I don't look like I've been smoking, do I?"

"You are smoking," Brady said. "Right now you are smoking."

"But I mean without the cigarette, you couldn't tell."

"Nuh-uh."

The wind shook the leaves of the willow tree. In the distance the car horn honked again.

"You know who else we have to definitely not tell," Koren said. "About this place."

"Who?"

"Is my stupid little brother."

"Eeeeeewwwwww."

"If he even breathed here like the trees would die. I'm not kidding."

"I know. If your little brother ever came here I'd puke."

✦   ✦   ✦

Brian stood at the entrance to the covered bridge, his dog tugging him forward. The road on the bridge's nether side was hard to see in the dark. Alex paused at the threshold and looked back up at Brian, unsure. Brian squinted into the darkness, listening for the thing he was more afraid of than anything else in the world: the sound of Mr. Bowman's voice whispering his name, calling to him, asking him to come along and be dead.

✦   ✦   ✦

Brian had appeared in one horse show only, the Brandywine Two-Day Event in Rose Tree. This was an exercise in public humiliation called Lead Line, designed, Brian deduced later, by girls in order to get boys out of the horse business as early as possible. In Lead Line, some woman pulled your pony around with a leash while you sat in the saddle and tried to look equestrian. There was some secret code of behavior no one would explain—something about posture and attitude, that, whatever it was, was unfathomable to Brian. He had lost Lead Line. There were only four girls in the class—all of them under the age of five—but, when the ribbons were given out, the girls had won everything. The boys were led out of the ring on their ponies, muttering, swearing they would never ride again, which, of course, was what the girls had planned all along.

✦   ✦   ✦

Brian's father had shown once as an open jumper, before the divorce. His horse was named Mysterious. The last time he had ridden Mysterious was a wet spring day at the Sugartown Horse Show; he had been approaching a set of double fences called the "in and out" when something had gone wrong. There was a shattering of wood, a horse's hoof knocking against a hollow wall, the deep crack of rails splitting, and the horrified inhalation of spectators.

Brian had missed his father's accident because he had been playing with GI Joe. He was vaguely aware of his father's presence in the ring, but he didn't watch. It was always the same. They went around and around in circles and then people applauded quietly, while he sat in the dust, in between the tailgates of cars parked out in a field, people walking by, cooling down their ponies, girls walking around in leather boots and cotton chokers, stable-mucking boys with bad teeth and transistor radios. The sun shone down on the dust, and Brian maintained a continuous monologue as GI Joe twisted back and forth. Joe would scale the rubber sides of a whitewall tire, look around at the top of the fender, then fall, screaming, into the yellow grass, where he'd lie unconscious, a victim of invisible Soviet zeltron rays. These were secret microwaves that could render one's life unnecessary.

Brian looked up to see his father flying through the air. Mysterious was on her knees, surrounded by broken rails. Father traveled face forward over the next jump, then angled down so that his final intersection with the earth took the form of a continuous roll. Then he lay still in the hot sun, clouds of kicked-up dust moving across the ring.

✦ ✦ ✦

Below the covered bridge, the waters of Crum Creek rushed over stones and the fallen limbs of evergreens. There were Canadian geese honking far overhead; squirrels and mice ran along the bridge's rafters. Before his death, Mr. Bowman had asked the class about heaven and hell. Most of the kids believed that when you died, that was it. The Kelehers were Catholic, but Brian didn't want to talk to the other kids about life after death. The afterlife was something most of them found hilarious.

Nancy Spellman had asked Mr. Bowman what he believed happened after you died. Mr. Bowman had said he thought your molecules went in all different directions—that part of you blew around in the air, and part of you went into the ground, and other bits merged with the parts of other people. At any moment it was possible that the molecules of lost Egyptian pharaohs were passing through you and merging with your spleen and lungs.

✦ ✦ ✦

In second grade Brian had been hit in the face with a baseball. He had been playing second base one day after his parents had spent the entire night screaming at each other. He had lain awake, looking at the ceiling.

The more he looked at the ceiling, the more it looked like the surface of the moon. He was an astronaut preparing for landing in the Sea of Fertility. This perspective made it necessary to invert gravity, of course, so that things were drawn upward, toward the mass of the moon ceiling. For a moment all would be quiet, and the room would be normal, then his parents would start fighting again, and gravity would be reversed and the ceiling would change into the Sea of Fertility. For a while it was interesting, in a sad way, but then when he tried to make the ceiling be itself again he found he was unable to change it back.

So he was tired the next day during the game and when Maynard Drier attempted to steal second he wasn't watching, and Tom Foulkrad, the pitcher, slammed a baseball toward Brian, whose eyes were closed. The ball bounced off Brian's lip, and he fell, in pain, into the dirt. Maynard Drier was safe.

✦   ✦   ✦

When Brian got home, his father took him into the backyard and started pitching baseballs at him. Something about "getting right back in the saddle," so as not to be afraid any more. Later, after Brian's father was thrown by Mysterious and had to give up riding, Brian wondered why no one forced his father to get back in the saddle. After all, the saddle his father had to get back into was not just a symbol of not being scared, but was a real saddle, so getting back into it seemed both logical and poetic. But after his flight his father never rode again, and Mysterious was sold to a man whose son was moving to Alaska. Mysterious was only five years old, but in horse years he was almost thirty-two. In dog years, the horse was forty-seven. They taught you how to figure out horse years and dog years in the cub scouts. It had something to do with life expectations.

✦   ✦   ✦

Mr. Keleher's new wife, Brenda, looked at her husband affectionately. He was staring at the mantelpiece, at the photograph of Koren and Jester, with Brian sipping his hot chocolate in the back. She leaned forward and kissed him on the neck, softly. The telephone rang.

✦   ✦   ✦

Brian and Alex were surrounded. Sound was different inside the bridge; things echoed. A board creaked beneath his foot. There was some graffiti spray-painted on the wall: U.S. Out of Toyland. Something moaned and croaked in the woods. There was a splash below; in summer there were water moccasins down there that sunned themselves on the rocks. They curled themselves up suddenly, angry, ready to inject their venom into an enemy they could not see. Brian thought about Mr. Bowman, and the way the ceiling in his room had become the Sea of Fertility.

✦ ✦ ✦

Koren had been currycombing Jester. The sunset had drained out of the clouds, leaving the sky pale and gray, with a small glow of bluish purple in the west. Jester stood in front of his stall, tethered to a clip on the side of the barn. Koren's mother was waiting in the car for her to finish.

Jester was dappled gray. Brady said Jester was a ghost horse because of his color. Above the stall was an old wasp's nest, left over from summer. Koren looked at it as she currycombed the pony. Her mother's cornball music played on a car radio, a Mitch Miller song. They used to watch that show: "Follow the bouncing ball." The whole family used to sit and watch it, and her father would make popcorn and they would eat it and drink ice water from a glass pitcher.

Jester reared up, as if stung by one of the bees from the dead hive. The lead line snapped, and the pony galloped away from the stable. He approached the ring, jumped over the fence. Koren chased after the pony, but could barely see him in the night. A headlight from a car shone off his gray flanks. He jumped over the far fence of the ring and disappeared.

✦ ✦ ✦

Brady walked toward Koren, and the two of them stood together by the old barn, listening to the pony fade. The sound of Jester's hooves was far away now, squashing in the soft mud of the far field. Brady was carrying a ribbon she was going to put in Jester's forelock. She wanted Koren to feel better even though she wasn't showing. Now Brady stood next to her friend, holding the ribbon in one hand.

Mrs. Keleher called to the girls and got them into the station wagon. Koren and Brady sat in the back seat, looking out into the night. Mrs. Keleher turned off the radio.

Koren's mother drove away from the barn, down the gravel road past the Kingman house. Kingman was standing on the porch with his dog, looking up toward the street. He began to walk across the far field, slowly at first, but then, hearing the terrible sound, broke into a run. Alex's father, Gomer, opened one eye and lifted his head.

✦ ✦ ✦

Brian stood in the middle of the covered bridge, looking into the distance. He and Alex were frozen, standing at the midpoint. Alex sniffed the air, as if he heard something. Brian felt the pull on the leash as he looked into the blackness. Now was the time. This was the moment Mr. Bowman would begin to speak.

✦ ✦ ✦

The road was already blocked off. Mrs. Keleher pulled over. "You two wait here," she told Koren and Brady. "I want you to stay here and don't move from this car under any circumstances, you understand?" Koren nodded slowly. "We'll stay," Brady said, holding her friend's hand. "We'll stay here." "It's my fault," Koren said. "I shouldn't have let him go. It's all my fault."

✦ ✦ ✦

The woman who was driving the car was not badly hurt, but she was crying and several of the stable boys had to hold her back. Her car, a yellow Barracuda, was ruined. Purple blood ran down the hood and onto the headlights. A group of men from the Rose Tree pony club was trying to move Jester out of the road. He glared at Mrs. Keleher with wide sad eyes. The vets were shooting him full of tranquilizers. An ambulance's beacon strobed orange across the faces of spectators. In the car Koren whispered to her friend. "I shouldn't have let him go," she said. "It's all my fault."

✦ ✦ ✦

Brian pulled on Alex's leash, and the dog relented. The two of them turned and walked out of the bridge. Brian thought about Mr. Bowman, and the quiz that he gave, and about floating breathatarians and getting hit in the face with baseballs. Most of all, though, he thought about his father flying through the air, and the sound of Mysterious crashing through the in and out. Behind them, in the rafters of the bridge, Mr. Bowman remained silent. It was getting late, and something was going on. Brian whistled to the dog. The two of them began to move through the darkness toward home, toward the single light in his sister's bedroom. An invisible Soviet zeltron ray passed silently over his head and disappeared.

✦ There's the Sea

Abbey met the very small man on board the U.S.S. *Bluenose* at eleven thirty, Atlantic time, fifty miles off the coast of Nova Scotia. He was standing in the front of the ship, looking out a porthole, tapping his foot. It wasn't clear whether he was humming some song to himself or if he was just nervous. Abbey sat down by a porthole, looked out on the Bay of Fundy, rested her chin on her hand. There was some song about the sea she could not remember. All the water makes me thirsty, Abbey thought. But the ocean is not good to drink.

The ocean was ten degrees Celsius, which was less than Fahrenheit. Abbey had twenty-eight Canadian dollars in her purse, which was either 32 percent more or 68 percent less than American money. A Canadian dollar was worth one thirty-five. So there's room for more cents in it. The twenty-eight dollars she had contained fewer of her large dollars but was actually worth more. The time in Newfoundland was an hour and a half ahead of Eastern time. This meant it was later there if you were in America looking east. The ocean temperature was something like one-third what it ought to be. Somewhere around here was where the *Titanic* sank.

"Are you from Canada?" Abbey said, unexpectedly. She figured he'd have to be.

The dwarf did not look at her. They were the only people in the observation deck, and yet he did not respond. Was he being rude? It wasn't certain that passengers were allowed up here; she had had to pass through a door that, although not exactly labeled Crew Only, did have a kind of official nautical look to it, and it was entirely likely that some seagoing person was going to pounce upon Abbey and the dwarf at any moment and throw the two of them into the brig together. You'd think this would have brought the two of them closer, but it didn't.

"Excuse me?" the dwarf said, turning to her. His head was remarkable. He had a wedge-shaped face, like a lump of clay, and piercing light blue eyes. The eyes were far apart, sunk into deep greenish hollows.

"From Canada. You. Are you?"

"Yeah," the dwarf said, matter of factly. "New Brunswick."

"Are you going on a vacation?"

The dwarf looked back out the window. "If you could call it that," he said, dejected.

A set of footsteps drew near—the clopping sound of a woman's low heels. Abbey could picture the woman the steps belonged to—prim, angry, wearing a coat that was too tight, a skirt with buttons. Suddenly she appeared: a cross woman in gray with a large hooked nose.

"Who's this you're talking to?" she said.

The dwarf looked out the window as long as he could. "I don't know," he said.

"I'm Abbey Melrose," Abbey said, standing.

The woman sized Abbey up.

"Come on," the woman said to the dwarf. "We're going to be late."

The dwarf put his hands on his knees and stared into the distance, as if he were a baseball catcher.

"Do you hear me?" the woman said. "We have to go. This instant. I'm serious, Arthur."

Arthur stood up, wiped his hands on his hips. The woman took him by the hand and escorted him down the hall. Abbey heard her footsteps clopping away, slower now to accommodate for Arthur's small stride.

This left Abbey all alone in the foredeck, and she stared out at the shoreline with some measure of self-pity. Cruises were supposed to be good places to meet people, but here she was abandoned again. Not that the dwarf was who she was intending to meet, but, if she couldn't even maintain a conversation with him, what could she expect? The ocean below looked like the skin of an elephant. How did that song go again?

It was almost a year ago when Abbey and this guy Deeno had had what they called their Festival Weekend. She had gone over to his house for dinner Friday night, and they drank three bottles of wine and talked about movies and their parents and being left-handed and things that were cursed and suddenly it was two in the morning and she was agreeing to spend the night with him. He had this great smell, like chocolate milk except more masculine. In the morning he had told her he thought he was falling in love with her and looked almost upset. They walked around New York that day, walked all the way from his house in the West Eighties down to the White Horse Tavern in the Village, looking at all the people and their attitudes. They had dinner that night at the Yun Luck

Rice House, and canoles in Little Italy. They had slept at Deeno's house again, and in the morning took a bath and read the Sunday *Times* in the tub. That evening they watched the Jerry Lewis telethon together, on which Julius LaRosa sang "I Guess I'm a Cockeyed Optimist," but that was not the song she was trying to recall now.

Deeno had not called back after that. She waited until Wednesday, then she called him, but there was only his answering machine, and she left a message, warm and cuddly, but he didn't call. She tried again Friday, but again only got the machine. It was just weird. Tried again Saturday, left a message much less cuddly, almost businesslike, as if it did not matter. He didn't call. What was the reason for that? Was it men in general or Deeno in particular? How can you read the paper in the tub with someone and then never call her again? Is that right?

It's me, Abbey concluded. That's what it is, is me. I have Loser written all over my face. I have a pointed nose. Something about it is off-center. Whenever men are nice to me, it's out of pity. Then the second I'm safely seen away, they run for their lives.

There's a hole in the bottom of the sea. That's it. A children's song. There's the sea, there's the sea, there's a hole in the bottom of the sea. Then the next verse is there's a bump on a log in the hole. Then there's a wart on the frog on the bump. It ends up with something like a newt on a germ on the hair on the wart on the frog on the bump on the log in the hole. There's the sea. Etc.

Something pink streaked by. Abbey looked up: someone had jumped overboard. She searched the waves for a human figure. Were they going too fast? Maybe she had already been swept under. What was it she had seen? Were her eyes playing tricks? There hadn't been a splash. Maybe the person was still falling.

There was a life preserver twenty feet down the deck. Abbey ran toward it but found it was wired to a kind of alarm device. If she threw the preserver, whistles would go off. What if there hadn't been anyone? They would stop the ship and go around in circles looking for a person that did not exist. The ferry would be late and people would point and they'd probably arrest her in Canada and throw her in some deep-woods jail.

But if there had been someone, she was the only one to have seen her, and even now precious seconds were escaping. Abbey might be killing her right now. She did not want to kill anyone, but neither did she wish to cause a scene.

"Miss?" a uniformed man said. He had a large black mustache and epaulets. "Are you all right?"

"I don't know," Abbey said. She looked back out on the sea. No one waved.

"I thought I saw something," she said, finally.

The admiral walked to the railing and surveyed the ocean. They were approaching two peninsulas that reached out from opposite sides of a bay like the points of calipers. He looked at the land, then at the sea.

"What did you think you saw?" he said.

"I don't know," Abbey said. "I'm not sure. I thought I saw somebody jump, or at least fly past. I didn't actually see them hit the water. It was like a brush of something, then it went away."

A brush of something? This was it. Abbey realized she sounded like a total idiot. This admiral has already consigned me to a realm inhabited by half-wits and circus freaks.

"What did it look like?" he said, evenly, patiently.

"Well, it was pinkish, or maybe a cream color. Like a yellowish pink, the color of those clouds."

She pointed toward the sky, but the admiral did not look. "Or the color of the dress you're wearing," he said.

He was right. Now it was final. She was having the kind of dream psychoanalysts would charge her for. Except most other people have theirs while they sleep, Abbey thought. I have to have mine out loud.

"It's a very nice color," the admiral said. "You look very beautiful in it."

This was not expected. There was only one explanation: the admiral himself was crazy. He was probably a fraud, some lunatic who had gotten on board in costume. But they wouldn't just let him parade around like that, would they? Didn't they check at the entrance, to see if people were impersonating sailors? Maybe he had changed once he got on board.

"It was probably just a gull," the admiral said. "The eyes can play tricks on you out here."

"Uh-huh," Abbey said. "Tricks."

"I hope you won't mind me asking this," he said. "But if you'd like to join me in my cabin for dinner, I would be honored."

"Dinner?" Abbey said. "Your cabin?"

"It's just that you looked so—how do I put it? Alone, out here, and that seems to me such a waste. A waste of a beautiful woman."

"Why thank you—uh, captain—."

"Lieutenant Smuggs. And you are—."

"Abbey. Abbey Melrose."

"Shall we say seven, then?"

"Thank you. I'm charmed. Really."

Lieutenant Smuggs saluted and walked down the promenade. Abbey looked out on the sea; the *Bluenose* had passed through the calipers and was now headed into the shoreless horizon. There was supposed to be lots of fog but there was none. "Shall we say seven, then?" There's a hole in the bottom of the sea.

At quarter past six, Abbey had tried on every article of clothing she had in her three suitcases. What did one wear to this sort of thing, anyway? It was a hard situation to call. If she showed up in something exceedingly casual, he might think she didn't care—and what if she arrived in pants and a shirt and there was the lieutenant in full military regalia, like the Prince of Wales or something? Or, conversely, she could wear one of the dresses she had brought with her, something she had bought exclusively for this vacation in the off chance that a situation exactly like the one she was now in presented itself. She could dress to the nines and prepare to swoop down on Lieutenant Smuggs like a carrion bird, only to find him in his cabin wearing a flannel shirt and a pair of dungarees he had obviously worn one day while painting the deck. She tried various combinations in an attempt to find something halfway between rare and burnt, but everything seemed slapdash, random, chaotic. At last she reached a kind of fury, an indecisive dementia in which every option was distasteful. She sat on the side of her bed in her slip and felt like she was losing her mind. Who was this Lieutenant Smuggs anyway? Had it been established that he was not a charlatan? If he was not a lunatic, the question remained, why in the world was he attracted to her? Maybe that was it, maybe he wasn't attracted to her and this was just his way of being gentlemanly. Was that possible? It was just pity? Abbey felt moisture in the hair above her temples.

She could not do it. She wanted so desperately to have dinner with Lieutenant Smuggs, a man who seemed to be everything she wanted, and yet knocking on his door was unthinkable. Once she was inside, safely drinking wine, laughing, that would be fine, but the presentation of the self, the standing on stage as the lights went up and the curtains parted— she would prefer never to have been born.

This is crazy, she thought. This is a wonderful chance. Why must I be such a coward? She looked at the pinkish beige dress she had been wearing in the afternoon. He liked that one. Why not come just as she had been? He liked me then. Why not pretend to be the same person as I was last time? Because, she thought, last time I wasn't the same person as I am now.

She got into bed and felt the ship rocking back and forth. Sometimes she got motion sickness, but not now. She had a book she did not read. Abbey reached over and turned off the light and bit down on her thumbnail and felt the ocean roll. She did not weep, but a single, continuous trickle of water seeped slowly from the eye nearest the pillow and spread into the pillowcase. Abbey made no sound.

She woke some time later to find a crack of light on one wall, the lieutenant's shadow midcrack. Abbey slept with her back to the door. Better to pretend she was asleep.

"Abbey?" the voice said.

"Come in," she said, "and shut the door."

"I finally got away," he said.

"I'm glad." He climbed into bed behind her, caressed her shoulder. His fingers were warm and smooth on her skin. She closed her eyes and felt him kiss her, gently, slowly. There's the sea, there's the sea, there's a hole in the bottom of the sea.

"I think that I am falling in love with you," he said.

She held his wedge-shaped face in her hands, looked into his deep-set, light blue eyes.

"I know," she said.

✦ Thirty-six Miracles of Lyndon Johnson

1.

The President is amazed by the stupidity of the King of Norway. "He [King Olaf] is the dumbest king I have ever met," the President says. "I didn't know they made kings that dumb."

2.

I am gathering an armful of wet wood for my wicked stepsister. Logs of sweet-smelling cherry are strewn on the front porch like damp jackstraws; a vile, gelatinous drizzle has turned the fallen snow into bad flan. The President died thirteen years ago this day; the wind-chill factor makes it feel like fifty. I can feel my mother watching me, the warmth of the house escaping through the door she holds open. The drenched logs leave gray stains on my pink shirt. "You lay those logs out on the floor of the bathroom," she says, "and I'll get Lucy to blow them with the hair dryer." The wood is from a cherry tree that fell last autumn. While we were splitting it, my stepfather got the wedge stuck in one of the logs; the only way to get the wedge out of the wood now is to burn it.

3.

The President has never liked the Lennons, and yet he is aware that he owes to them his place in history. He cannot bring himself to say "Jack." When he must refer to Lennon by name, his face contracts as if rolled-up balls of aluminum foil are grinding between his molars and his fillings. He does not read newspapers that feature Yoko on the cover.

4.

Sean Ono Kennedy is seven today. The President has sent him a comb. "First time anyone in that family ever owned one," he says. "Stupid-ass sons of bitches."

5.

My mother and I are sitting around a table with claws for feet. All of my stepfather's things are lying askew where he left them. He still receives mail. The kitchen window opens onto a field covered with melting snow. The windmills at Anderosson Farms should be visible in the distance, but the fog obscures them. My mother and I are eating leftover Roy Rogers fried chicken. "Your brother,"she says. "He's the only one still in the dark." From upstairs comes the whine of the blow-dryer.

6.

Dear Sean:
    It will be many years before you understand fully what a great man your father was. His loss is a deep personal tragedy for all of us, but I wanted you particularly to know that I share your grief—
    You can always be proud of him.

Affectionately,
Lyndon B. Johnson

7.

I am sitting at the baby grand piano in the living room. When my father was twelve, he heard Artur Rubenstein at the Academy of Music in Philadelphia. As he gazed down from the Family Circle—Rubenstein's hair like the greens of distant carrots—his head was encircled by phantoms of amazement. His glands secreted juices. Chopin's *Etudes*. The *Pavone for a Dead Princess*. *The Moonlight Sonata*. Mendelssohn's *Fantasia in A Minor*. *With the Dead in a Dead Language* by Mussorgsky. He sobbed silently as each note revealed to his mind the limitless topography of a new and unknown planet.

8.

The President: "He got on top of me and he put his body between me and the crowd. He had his knees in my back and his elbows in my back and a good two hundred pounds all over me. And the car was speeded up. He had a microphone from the front seat that he'd pulled over with him, a two-way radio, and there was a lot of traffic on the radio and you could hear them talking back and forth, and one of them said, 'Let's get out of here quick.' The next thing we were on the way to the hospital."

9.

My mother collects stamps from foreign countries in an album abandoned by my father at age twelve. That's when the piano lessons be-gan. There are magenta squares, orange triangles, strange flags on perforated trapezoids. While she sits in her study and pastes in her stamps with a special glue, she hums a tuneless tune to herself. The song has no title. Its words are: *They all moved over and one fell out: there were three in the bed and the little one said: roll over.* My mother can play this song on the piano as long as she makes no errors. If she misses a note, she has to stop, gather her wits, and start over again from the beginning. When she does this, my stepsister and I look on, drinking gin, encouraging her with our amused and agonized politeness.

10.
My wicked stepsister has grown weary of blow-drying the cherry and has placed the logs inside an electric blanket. "She's crazy," she says. "This wood is made of stuff which does not burn." Lucy doesn't like extremes of taste and smell. A toasted marshmallow is enough to send her to the hospital. "Ants," she says, pointing toward the cherry. The logs, all snug in the master bedroom, are riddled with bullet holes. "Carpenter ants. That's why the tree fell."

11.
Lady Bird: "I went looking for Yoko and ran into her smack like that. She was still in pink. She reached out to my face as if it were a mirror, then said: 'Are you still here?' She sounded annoyed."

12.
A secret service agent came into the room. Some senators, a well-known actress, two governors, and the Maharishi were seated in chairs. The President stood up. The agent said, "He's gone."

13.
The President: "The greatest shock that I can recall was one of the men saying: 'He's gone.' "

14.
Yoko: "If you become naked . . . "

15.
Lucy: "Mother said she was going to write him." "I know. But he's closer to me. He'll want to hear it from me." "Tell him I have a friend in the Peace Corps who got bowed and arrowed." "I'm sure he's aware of

the risks." "He's not aware of anything. You're all alike." She ruffles her feathers by the fireplace. "Can you move? Your shadow's blocking the heat." She looks at me. "What's wrong with you? Can't you take a hint?" Timidly: "It's not your fire, anyway."

16.

My mother surrounds herself with the stamp collection, her colorful triangles, a sponge dampened in an ashtray filled with water. You can tell which stamps were affixed by my mother; they're the ones that aren't straight. Sometimes she puts stamps in the wrong places on purpose. My stepfather was angered by this enterprise. "Why are you keeping his collection going?" he'd say. "He's dead. You could be doing something new." "I like looking at the pictures," she'd say. "Places where it's a different time than ours." Whenever she had a falling out with my stepfather, she turned to the album as the one thing that was her own.

17.

This is a sad time for all people. We have suffered a loss that cannot be weighed. For me it is a deep personal tragedy. I know that the world shares the sorrow that Mrs. Lennon and her family bear. I will do my best. That is all I can do. I ask for your help—and God's.

18.

I am sitting at the baby grand piano. I begin to pick out random chords. E minor, then D major, then E minor again. E minors replaced by alternating D majors and B minor sevenths. When my stepfather was drunk, he would ask me to play "I Write The Songs." "I don't know it," I'd say. My stepfather used to drink gin from the cap of the bottle it came in. "You should."

19.

Paul McCarthy: "It wasn't like what you read. We'd do stuff together now and then. He'd write the middle eight. Or I'd write his. We were always superseding each other. Like in 'Day in the Life.' That whole middle part—'Woke up, got out of bed, dragged a comb across my head.' That was all Lyndon's. I think he was trying to make fun of Jack. You know it was an obsession of his. How none of them ever seemed to have a comb. It was just this thing of his. He was strange that way."

20.

Jack: "We are the biggest thing since Jesus Christ."

21.

[I.e.: 1. Raising of the widow's son (Paul 7:11); 2. Passing unseen through the multitude (Paul 4:30); 3. Healing the nobleman's son (John 4:46); 4. The dumb man healed (Ringo 7:31); 5. Stilling of the storm (Ringo 4:37); 6. Curing the demonic child (George 17:24) . . . etc., etc.]

22.

Hours are consumed with the preliminaries of communication. I'm using the special writing paper, the cream-colored stock bearing my stepfather's initials. I have gone through drawers looking for the right pen with which to write words of sorrow. I have found photographs, paper clips, report cards, a book of tiny, gummed address labels, photographs from a trip to a wax museum. I write the word: Dear—and draw a few triangles with the pen. I check the clock: it is late. In a few moments it will be tomorrow. Across the Atlantic it is almost dawn.

23.

[An aide:] "He was a weasel. That's all I remember. He had those enormous ears and everything and I think he felt he had to prove to women he wasn't as ugly as they thought. I remember one night I was staying at the Ranch in Texas when suddenly I felt this enormous person in the bed next to me—and you know he was gigantic—when he lay down it was like being in bed with an ocean liner—and I hear this voice say: 'Ask not what your country can do for you; ask what you can do for your country.' Then he laughed that Texas laugh of his: 'Haw de-haw de-haw.' "

24.

[An aide:] "It was the night after they did the (Ed Sullivan Show.) The group had flown into Chicago, and Jack and I went out to the lakefront and drank from some bottle of something he was carrying around. There was a smell in the air like it was going to rain. He talked about his brother Joe—the one who was killed in the war. Talked about how Joe held his head under water in a swimming pool when they were kids. Jack got angrier and angrier as he talked about it. I think he hated his older brother, even twenty years later. It started to rain—I mean really pour—

and we ran, screaming—into this apartment on Michigan Avenue where one of his women lived. We begged for dry clothes; she looked at him with the look of someone who knows she's unable to refuse an unreasonable request. She put our clothes in the dryer, and Jack and I stood around naked with this girlfriend of his, listening to our clothes rotate. She got us some beer. At last she offered us some clothes—they were the things of her eight-year-old son—and went back to bed. Jack and I sat around drinking, waiting for our clothes to dry, wearing these cub scout uniforms. That was the last time I saw him. I loved him. He was the best friend I ever had. I loved him like a brother."

25.

George: "He wasn't very bright, now was he? It took him like a year and a half to learn all the songs. If the Stones hadn't been in jail—and the ones that weren't in jail weren't working day and night trying to teach Goldwater the Brian Jones licks—they would have gotten the better of us. Goldwater was the only thing worse than Johnson, when you think about it now. Whenever I have me bad memories, I just think of Goldwater singing 'Ruby Tuesday,' and I cheer up a little bit. Not much though."

26.

The President: "The attorney general called me from Liverpool. He felt that the oath should be taken in Dallas, immediately. I said, 'Well we don't have the oath here. Nobody knows what it is.' He said, 'I think I can find it. We've got it around here someplace.' There we were, trapped in Dallas, and nobody had the oath. So somebody in Liverpool found a copy of it and read it over the phone and we wrote it down with a Bic pen on the back of a piece of waxed cardboard that had come on the bottom of a package of cupcakes and that was it."

27.

Early in the morning I write furiously to my older brother. It has all come at once. "When I was younger, that is, not as old as I am now, old friend, which is to say, when I was younger than I am on this particular day, I never needed anyone's assistance, not in any way. Now, on the other hand, those days are gone, and now I find I change my opinion on things all the time. It's like a door opening. Let us both give each other assistance at this time, if we can, for I am certain that you are feeling as down as I am. I do appreciate the fact that you have always been there for me. Perhaps we can both get our feet back on planet Earth together. Let us both try to help each other."

28.

The President awakes one night in the spring of 1968, screaming in Jack's voice. Outside there are protestors in Lafayette Park. The President is sitting up in bed. Lady Bird: "I came into his room at about two in the morning and found him with his hands outstretched; he was shaking them violently in front of his head. He was screaming the same thing over and over: 'I got blisters on me fingers!' "

29.

"When are you leaving?" my stepsister asks. "Soon. After the funeral." The fire, my stepsister, and I are in eclipse formation. "He missed the last one, too." "Who?" "My brother. He was already in Africa." "I've never met him." "He's nice." The fire is beginning to billow smoke into the room; she looks tense, sniffing the air. There is a sudden metallic clank, like a blacksmith's hammer pounding a horseshoe. The wedge has fallen out of the burning cherry onto the hearth. It lies there, glowing red. "Jesus Christ!" my stepsister says, waving her hands in front of her face. "Can't we open some windows in here?"

30.

I learned how to play "I Write the Songs." My stepfather would fall asleep listening to me play. He would snore. The part of the piano that swings back to uncover the keys—the part with "Steinway" printed on it—is sliced with the faded scratches of my father's fingernails. I once asked him why he never played anymore. We were visiting colleges in the Midwest in my senior year of high school; we had visited Northwestern during the day and were now drinking together—perhaps really getting drunk together for the first time as father and son—in a restaurant in the Hilton. "When I was growing up they told me I would be a concert pianist," he said. "I got better and better until I reached a certain point. I stopped there. I was good enough to know what I ought to be doing better, but not good enough to do it. So I stopped. There was no joy in ruining Beethoven." By the time I was a freshman at Northwestern he was dead. My mother remarried the following year. It was exam week.

31.

There is a sound of a television on in my mother's study. It is the sound of the Tonight Show. Tommy Newsom is filling in for Doc. Doc is filling in for Ed. Ed is filling in for Joan Rivers. Joan Rivers is filling in for Johnny. Johnny is on vacation.

32.

[An aide:] "Naturally there was a great deal of animosity between the Johnson faction and the McCartney faction. When McCartney got 42 percent of the vote in New Hampshire—and then four days later Julian threw his hat into the ring—it was the sounding of a dirge for the President. He had grown weary of it all. He had spent the best years of his life in the Beatles; had often threatened to leave, had even decided, irrevocably, to do so, only to be asked by McCartney to hold off the announcement until after the convention. Then to have McCartney steal his fire like that—well, it got under the President's skin. He came back to the White House kitchen and ate nine gallons of chili and sat in front of the television and watched the news and stank up the Lincoln Room. He was an odious man: vile, disgusting, humongous."

33.

My mother sits at her roll-top desk. She has cut the stamps off of the envelope I have addressed to my brother and is pasting them in her collection. Four American flags fly on the pages of the Democratic Republic of Togo. "Did you think he'd get the letter," she asks vacantly, "even if you did mail it?" "I don't know, Ma." "He never writes back. How do we know he's not dead?" "He isn't. I'm sure of it." She closes the album. "I'm old, honey," she says. "I'm not worth ten cents." There is a window above her desk which looks out on the melting fields, the broad hill leading toward the neighbor's windmill. "You ought to take this." She pushes the old binder toward me. "Your father always wanted your brother to have it. I've got some other things of his, too. I've been saving them for him. A tea box and some scissors. Things from his boyhood." She stretches her fingertips toward me, as if she is feeling for me in the dark. "I want you to have them." We embrace; my mother cries silently in the folds of my pink shirt. "Oh, honey," she says, "I'm old."

34.

[An aide:] [It was the night he told the country he wasn't going to run again. We were discussing the speech.] "He said he had an ending of his own to add to mine, and I told him I wasn't surprised. He asked me if I had any idea what he'd say. I said I thought I did and he wanted to know what I thought of it. I said something like, 'I'm very, very sorry, Mr. President.' He sort of smiled and said, using his most Texas accent, 'Well, so long pardner,' and he left."

35.

My mother asks me to play Mussorgsky at my stepfather's funeral. I will do my best. That is all I can do. I ask for your help—and God's.

36.

Jack, hair askew, smile triumphant, waves to a crowd from the open car. "Thank you on behalf of the group and ourselves, and I hope we pass the audition."

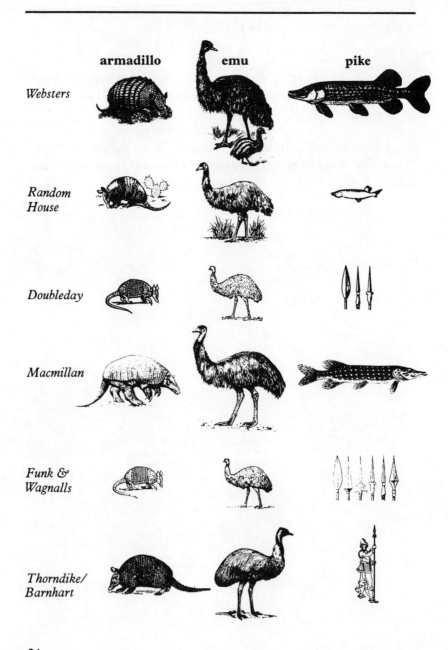

	armadillo	emu	pike
Websters			
Random House			
Doubleday			
Macmillan			
Funk & Wagnalls			
Thorndike/ Barnhart			

dic·tion·ar·y art re·view (dik′ shə ner′ē art ri vyōō), *n.* **1.** a comparative examination of the drawings that illustrate dictionaries. **2.** pictures that the world would be a more confused place without. **3.** something for the little guy. **4.** a random selection that substitutes missing images where necessary because some dictionaries didn't include that which all the other dictionaries thought important to include.

metronome	eagle	fangs	buggy

No metronome, but here's their bib.

No eagle. Here's a flying squirrel.

day (dā), *n.* [ME fr. OE *doeg* dog + OE *yister* yesterday = "dog-time"]: **1.** when it gets light until when it gets dark. **2.** rotation of earth ("have a nice ~ ").

dead (ded), *adj.* [ON *dauthr* extremely tired]: **1.** what you wind up. **2.** croquet: temporarily forbidden from play. **3.** obsolete (a ~ language) **4.** doomed (a ~ duck).

dead-man's float (ded' manz'), *n.:* **1.** a way of swimming that attracts a lot of attention at first but eventually they find out you're only faking and then they throw you out of the pool. **2.** a confection made with two scoops of vanilla ice cream, chocolate syrup, poison, and club soda.

Deb·or·ah (deb' ər ə), *n.:* **1.** a: Hebrew prophetess who aided the Israelites in their early struggles against the Canaanites. b: a friend of mine who got Hodgkin's disease. She had one green eye and one blue one, like Tommy Smothers. We had to give her white blood cells because her body stopped making them. Once we spent a night and an afternoon in an abandoned radio station but later, when I asked her about it, she couldn't remember and it was as if it had never happened.

de·caf·fein·ate (dē kaf'ə nāt'), *v.t.* [*de* + ME *kavus* to strike with lightning]: to take the zip out of.

dé·colle·tage (dā kol täzh'), *n.* [GER *deco* modern + Indian *kola* soft + *taj* onion]: We were in that old radio station sitting by the rusted transmitter. She had lost a lot of weight since her first transfusion but now she looked better, like I was with somebody new. I was wondering, because she had all new blood now, if the kind of things she thought might be affected by the thoughts of the blood donors. Like the things she thought now were different because the blood in her veins had been produced by other people. Including me, because I had donated some while she was sick. There was this frog or something behind the transmitter. I thought how strange that she wanted to kiss me now and she hadn't before, because now she had a pint of my blood in her and it was enough to tip the scales in her brain, like having a liberal judge replace a conservative one on the Supreme Court, only from the inside. She kissed me with a soft abrasive tongue, which reminded me of her sister, Molly. I think it was a family thing. Bloodwise, Molly was a universal recipient, opposite of me.

deep′six′ (dēp′ siks′), *n.:* sailor's slang for "burial at sea." Probably from the tradition of burying the dead six feet down, at least when they're horizontal.

de·gust (di gust′), *v.t.* [OE *glestus* gland]: to taste or savor.

dé·jà vu (dā zha vy′), *n.* [F, viewed twice, like Zsa Zsa]: A few weeks later I was sleeping with Deborah's sister, Molly, who had hair that went way up over her head like Katherine Hepburn, and the phone started ringing and I could tell it was Deborah calling. It was the timing of the silence between the rings that tipped me off. So I let it ring and ring but she didn't hang up, and soon it started interfering with our lovemaking. I mean how can you concentrate with a phone ringing and everything, so I made Molly sit up and I picked up the phone and hung it up again but the phone started ringing again so I went over and yanked the cord out of the back of the phone. Then we were just left looking at each other and I started thinking about Deborah and how I really did love her in a way, and I went into the kitchen and put some water on and Molly came in, putting her hair back up, and asked me if I wanted her to leave. She was nice about it. I had some tea and thought about how I am kind of a scuzzball if you think about it and I plugged the phone back in and it immediately started ringing again. I said hello, but there was nobody there—nothing except a distant radio, maybe somebody banging pots and pans around in a sink. I think it was as if she had called me and had not hung the phone up the right way so it just kept ringing. I tried hanging up on her but every time I plugged in the phone for the next day it rang and I heard her in her house, unaware that I could hear her breathing, humming to herself, rustling in her covers. Later I tried calling her from a pay phone but the line was busy and by the time it wasn't busy any more she wasn't answering.

del·i·quesce (del′ə kwes′), *v.i.* [L *delivere* remove the liver aspect from + L *liquere* with a fluid attitude]: **1.** to melt away: a: to dissolve gradually and become liquid by attracting and absorbing moisture from the air. b: to become soft or liquid with age.

de·lir·i·um (di lēr'ē əm), *n., pl.* [L *delirare* to be crazy, + E, Edward Lear]: **1.** mental disturbance; confusion. **2.** frenzied joy.

de·liv·er (di liv' ər), *v.t.* [OF *delivere* remove liver from]: **1.** to set free. **2.** to hand over. **3.** to assist in giving birth. **4.** to tell a story, relate.

de·lu·sion (di loo' zhən), *n.* [MF *lavere* + Chin. *Chun* to wash mind with mud]: the act of deluding; something that is believed for all the wrong reasons.

de·men·tia (di men'shə), *n.* [L *demens* + Chin. *Chun* devil + mind-mud]: The next time there was a bunch of us—me and Molly and Molly's ex-boyfriend Chris and some others, and they took us all into a room to get our white blood cells because that seemed to be the problem. They removed a pint of our blood and then took it away and spun it around in a centrifuge. We sat in these chairs, about ten of us in a starlike formation, our feet touching like we were dancers in a Busby Berkeley picture. They kept the holes in our arms open by giving us a saline solution. It was cold and you could feel the coldness pulsing all over your body. When it reached your heart, it was as if your insides had turned to some kind of liquid metal. I kept thinking of Deborah the whole time though it hurt a great deal. Chris was in the chair next to me and he turned to me at one point and asked me why I thought Deborah should want my cells. I just looked at him and felt the pain of the needle and he said, Bastard, you bastard, and then the nurse came in and took the saline solution away and we got our own blood back. It was warm, strange to be filled up with your own blood, like filling a water balloon from a faucet. I kept trying to make eye contact with Molly, to exchange a glance with her to make the moment special but she was out cold. Chris just asked the nurse if Deborah was all right and looked at me and the nurse and said, Just make sure the blood I get back is my own.

de·ny (di nī'), *v.t.* [*de* + E *Nilech* to flow in the opposite direction (as the Nile)]: **1.** to give a negative answer. **2.** to refuse to accept the facts.

de·sire (di zī ˀr'), *n.* [E *dezz* to look toward + L *sidus* star]: **1.** longing, craving. **2.** a formal request for some action.

de·spair (di spâr'), *v.i.* [*de* + L *sperare* to hope]: to lose all hope or confidence.

de·Sta·lin·i·za·tion (dē stȝ'li ni za' ṣhən), *v.t.*: the deflation of Stalin and his policies.

de·tick (di tik'), *v.t.*: to remove ticks from.

de·tri·tus (di trī'təs), *n.* [F *Detrich* to make someone (esp. a professor) crow like a rooster]: loose material that results directly from disintegration.

dev·il-may-care, *adj.*: reckless, brash, informal.

di·aph·a·nous (dī af'ə nəs), *adj.* [ML *diapainein* to show through]: The last time I saw her I held her hand for a while, read her the paper. She kept waking up and falling asleep. She was off the platelets by then. I kissed her, waking her, pressed her hand, and she coughed. I said, you know, we'll always have that night in the radio station, and she looked confused and said she didn't know what I was talking about but that she was glad I was there. She asked me how Molly was and I said fine. The phone started ringing and ringing and finally I answered and it was Chris. Deborah smiled when she found out it was him and I left her there talking on the phone, the sun slanting through the window, light crossing above her bed and falling on the opposite wall.

di·as·to·le (dī as't ᵊlē'), *n.* [G *stellen* to send fluid to someone]: a rhythmic expanding, esp. the swelling of the cavities of the heart until they fill with blood.

di·ath·e·sis (dī at̲h̲' i sis), *n.* [OE "die-at-the-sea"]: an attitudinal predisposition toward an abnormality.

di·a·tribe (di'ə trib), *n.* [OE *die* + Am. Ind. *a tribe*]: an unexpected, usually overlong piece of abusive speech or writing.

di·chot·o·my (dī kot'ə mē), *n.* [L *dios* god + E *kados* bisection of]: **1.** the phase of the moon, or an inferior planet in which half its disk appears illuminated. **2.** repeated bifurcation or forking.

dic·tion·ar·y (dik' ṣhə ner'ē), *n.* [OE *dictator* + Fr *canary*]: a reference work listing alphabetically terms or names important to a particular subject or activity along with names and applications in one language giving equivalents in another.

Di·do (dī'dō), *n.* [Gk *Deido*]: a queen of Carthage in the *Aeneid* who entertains Aeneas, falls in love with him and, on his departure, stabs herself.

did·y·mous (did'ə məs), *adj.* [Gk *didymos* double, twin]: growing in pairs, twins.

die (dī), *v.i.* [ON *deyja* to see the end]: **1.** what is shaken, what we must do, what is cast. **2.** stop.

✦ The Gissix Project

I first became aware of gissix when my neighbor Edward Bickford accidentally ran a lawn mower over his nephew's box turtle. I had been sitting on the back porch of my house, reading, when I suddenly heard the distinctly unpleasant crunch. I smiled, for Bickford, to be frank about it, is an idiot, and my family considers anything that plagues his afternoon to be God's way of encouraging Bickford to move. Moments later, however, I heard him actually sobbing. The engine of the mower sputtered and died. Reluctantly, I got up and walked over to the fence that divides our properties.

Bickford sat on the seat of his tractor, holding his face in his hands. I could see tears running through the spaces between his fingers. Because Bickford is not particularly lachrymose (except when he hears the melody to "The Island of Misfit Toys"), I was touched, sort of.

"Hey, Bickford," I said. "Do you want to talk about it?"

He looked up at me, shook his head, and continued to weep.

"Hey," I said. "Ed."

He moaned. "My maw . . . " he blubbered.

"What about her?"

He shrugged. "She was so . . . good."

I climbed over the fence and placed a hand on my neighbor's shoulder. "Of course she was," I said, feeling that this was what was needed. "Of course she was good."

As I was saying these words, a strange nostalgia swept over me. I felt captive to a forgotten fragrance, the smell of brown bread baking on an autumn day in the late 1940s. As I consoled Bickford, I could not help thinking about my own mother, a tired woman whom I always think of as laughing, crinkles in the corners of her eyes.

I sat down next to Bickford's tractor and began to weep. Memories surfaced. That time my mother swam into the middle of Lake Erie to rescue Pinky. The annoying song she used to play on the piano. The time we went to Williamsburg and I locked her in the stocks. Why are children so cruel? Why aren't adults better adjusted?

At six o'clock our wives got back from the club and found the two of us sitting in the backyard. Mrs. Bickford brought her nephew Timmy with her. Timmy, surveying the wreckage, immediately detected the presence of what had been Knuckles, the turtle. Timmy picked up the sundered halves of Knuckles and ran, crying, back into the house. The women, who were just about to burst into tears themselves—Mrs. Bickford was already beginning to sing "Make New Friends but Keep the Old"—suddenly placed their hands on their hips and demanded to know "this very instant" what we two men thought we were up to. Bickford and I came to our senses and, with the air of two men who have unintentionally shared a great intimacy, immediately took leave of each other, self-conscious and embarrassed.

The next day, when Knuckles was buried beneath the mailbox post, all four adults—the Bickfords, my wife, Judy, and myself— again found themselves weeping, surrounded, as it were, by the long-lost fragrances of childhood. With a sudden inspiration, I understood that the odor I was smelling was not the scent of my mother's bread, but that of Knuckles himself. I carried his corpse back to our basement and sealed it up in a plastic bag. It took some time to convince my friends—let alone Timmy—that my actions were in the best interests of science.

Two weeks later, according to the biochemical researchers at the Department of Defense, the facts were these: Knuckles was no ordinary turtle, but a much rarer *Prussea tortae*, the "Prussian turtle," thought to have been extinct since the First World War. The process of grinding the turtle's shell at a certain point in its existence apparently releases a natural but extremely uncommon gas known as gissix. Gissix, according to the Department of Defense, has the unusual quality of being able to establish a link in the brain between the olfactory system and the long-term memory. In short, gissix, in certain quantities, gives its victims the illusion that the smells of their childhoods have been returned to them.

The effects of gissix were quite simple to gauge. Five men and five women were placed in a room literally reeking with ground-up *Prussea tortae*. Three of the men said the smell resembled the ground pencil shavings and floor wax of their elementary schools. Two of the women and one of the men said gissix smelled like boiling cabbage. Two more women said it was the smell of chocolate cake. One man said it smelled like his half-brother, who put water instead of milk on his cereal, and the other woman said it was the exact smell of the rain on the window of a house with a dirt floor. All ten subjects left the room in tears.

A partial examination of gissix in history ensued. To the presence of the Prussian turtle in the area surrounding Berlin was traced the kaiser's unexpected melancholy of 1916. Likewise Abraham Lincoln's son Tad is known to have kept several box turtles in the White House basement, and there is proof now not only that these were *Prussea tortae* but also that these are directly related to the sixteenth president's legendary inability to loosen up. And of course Marcel Proust practically survived on turtle soup, giving credence to the theory that entire chapters of *Remembrance of Things Past* have less to do with artistry and more to do with a man who has thoroughly saturated his synapses with the seething catnip of ground-up reptile.

That the mournfulness of childhood recaptured could ever be considered an agent of death only indicates the ingeniousness of certain quarters of the Pentagon. Three months after the division of Knuckles, enough of these creatures had been gathered and slaughtered to make a kind of experimental pseudo-bomb. The image of battlefields of Russian soldiers throwing down their arms and weeping for forgotten bowls of potato-leek soup was too much to resist, and soon thereafter a demonstration of the "Memory Bomb" was scheduled at the Bonneville Salt Flats, outside of Salt Lake City.

On the dawn of the day in question, a thick mist hung over the desert. The plain was deserted except for the top military brass, the scientists connected with the project, the president, and the Bickfords, who had threatened to make the details public if they were not invited. At zero hour, the horizon turned pink. I thought of the lines of Wordsworth: "The child is father of the man / And I could ask my days to be / Bound each to each by natural piety." I thought of my mother teaching me how to tell time.

Bickford and I began to sob immediately. The generals looked at us in surprise, as if we were trying to pull something over on them.

"This is supposed to bring back the smell of . . . what?"

"Childhood," muttered a CIA man.

"Well hell," said the secretary of defense. "My childhood didn't smell like much. Homework, that's about it."

"Mine smelled like plaid," said one of the joint chiefs of staff. "Hell, what does plaid smell like?"

"Is it over?" the CIA man said. "Was that it, or is there more?"

The top brass shrugged their shoulders as Bickford and I wept bitterly.

The directors of the project, who were wearing gas masks, were about to send everyone home, when a small tear was noticed on the president's nose.

He sniffed. "My maw . . . " he said.

"What about her?" said the secretary of defense.

"My maw . . . " the president tried again.

"Come on now, spit it out, Mr. President."

"My poor old maw . . . "

"Please, nail it down, sir."

"She . . . she would of done anything for me."

The president covered his eyes, and the secretary of defense and the joint chiefs of staff averted theirs, embarrassed and annoyed.

The test was considered a success, and yet, as everyone knows by now, the test itself doomed the "Memory Bomb" to failure. The directors had set off the bomb to prove it was possible; unfortunately, they had also used all the remaining *Prussea tortae* in developing the weapon. Now, given the go-ahead to mass-produce "turtle bombs," the scientists found the raw material inexplicably exhausted. A search for more of the tortoises has yielded only snappers and guppies. One of the directors almost lost a finger trying to bisect a snapper, and said that he would just as soon drop all this and get back to the Strategic Defense Initiative and the blowing up of nuns and orphans from space.

And that's where the matter stands today. There are reports, unverified, that the Russians have developed a kind of horseshoe crab that gives off the nervous fragrance of middle age. There is also the matter of the Pennsylvania sea horse, which, although devoid of smell, is said to have the ability to make people think someone from high school is calling from the next room. Its defensive capabilities are unknown.

For my part, next time Bickford runs over something with his tractor, I'm going to keep reading. His nephew got a pet rabbit two weeks ago; three days later Bunny had been eaten by a Dalmatian. We had a funeral for the rabbit, complete with a cigar-box casket and my daughter playing "Beautiful Dreamer" on the flutophone.

We all stood around and cried.

✦ Weasels

The man comes in. He's got the hose. It's attached to a large brass tank.

"Understand you've got weasels," he says.

"It's my wife who's seen'em," I say.

"Is she in?"

He gives a half-grin, switches the hose to the other hand.

"Is who in?"

"Your wife."

"Listen," I say, but he doesn't.

"You said she saw'em," he says.

"She's asleep," I say.

"Well, can you wake her up?" he says. "I've got the spray."

"I would but—." I put on my glasses. "She only just got to bed. See, she gets up early in the morning. She's trying to get her balloonist's license. That's when the winds are best. In the morning, I mean."

He starts pumping a handle on the tank up and down, working up a sweat. "Gotta keep this stuff under pressure," he says.

"Or what?"

"What do you mean?"

"Or what happens? If it's not under pressure?"

He shrugs. "I don't know." He looks at his watch. "So when do you think she's getting up?"

"I can show you where they were."

"I thought you said you hadn't seen'em."

"I can show you where she said she saw them."

He's picked up a framed photo from the piano. "This her?"

"Yes," I say. "That's her."

"Where was this taken?"

"I don't know. Halloween party. A few years back. A lot of years back."

From the next room comes the sound of something hitting the floor. Maybe her hand, hitting the hardwood.

"What's she supposed to be here?"

"Anna Karenina," I say.

"Huh," he says, putting the photo back on the piano. "Looks kind of like what's her name."

"Who?"

"I don't know. Some woman." He lifts the tank. "You smell something in here?"

"No," I say.

"Maybe it's you. You know how some people have a smell." He starts walking toward me, sniffing. "Nah. It's not you. Funny smell though. Like smoke."

He looks at his watch again. "Might as well start." He starts to spray around the kitchen: behind the stove, around the sink, in the garbage.

"No," I say. "They're out back." I'm pointing toward the bedroom. "I can show you where she saw'em."

He doesn't look up. "They feed in here," he says.

The stuff that comes out of the tank is a dense blue fog.

"What is that stuff?"

"Poison," he says.

From the bedroom, I hear something crash again, and then Nadine's voice. It sounds like she's laughing, covering her face with the pillow to keep me from hearing her.

"Maybe I should just wake Nadine," I say. "I'm sure she won't mind."

"No, no," he says. The guy's opening up the cupboard, spraying the plates and saucers. "You let her sleep. If she's all tuckered out you don't want to wake her. Probably just yell, you know how they are."

He puts the hose down, reaches into his uniform, puts on a white surgical mask.

"Is that necessary?" I say.

"It's poison," he says.

"Maybe I should open some windows," I say.

He looks at me and shakes his head. "And let it out?" he says.

"Well, that's where they are," I say.

"Yeah," he says, and I can see he's losing patience. "But they feed in here." He's opening the refrigerator, spraying the milk cartons and the orange juice and the Tupperware containing the leftover Chinese food and the frozen peas in the freezer and the Jell-O Pudding Pops and the Scooter Pies. The cloudlike poison passes from topmost shelf to lowermost shelf and is divided by the steel rungs of the shelves in such a way that it resembles a hard-boiled egg passing through an old-fashioned wire egg slicer.

"Do you want me to get the food out of there?" I say.

"It's not my house," he says. "You do what you want."

I'm starting to get a headache. "Is that stuff toxic?" I say. "I'm feeling kind of discombobulated."

"You have a good breakfast?" he says. "That can make a big difference. Most important meal of the day."

"No, the stuff in the tank," I say. "Is it toxic?"

He's opening up my desk drawers, spraying the gas in there. He's going through my letters, half-ideas scratched on legal pads, report cards from elementary school.

"You mean like toxic waste? No. It's not like that," he says. "Not as long as you keep it under pressure."

"What happens if you don't keep it under pressure?"

"You want I should find out?"

It's getting harder to see him; the place is beginning to fill up with the thick, bluish fog.

"Hey, look at this," the man's voice says.

I can't see what he's got.

"What have you got there?" I say.

"More pictures of your wife," he says. "I guess it's her. Man, oh man. I'll bet she knows how to pin the tail on the ol'donkey, you know what I'm sayin'?"

"Where are you?"

"I'm in front of you. I'm standing right here. Are you all right?"

"No, I'm not. I'm tired. I think I have to lie down."

"I don't mind."

The place is filled with fog now. It's getting harder and harder to think straight. I try licking some of the cloud juice off of my thorax or whatever you call it, but it just makes my tongue taste funny, like machine oil.

"I'm going to do your wife's room now," he says, and pads off down the hallway. "Hey you know who she looks like? I figured it out. That woman on the shuttle. The one that blew up. Not Sally Ride, but the other one. You know."

I once saw a movie of them sleeping on the *Discovery*; her hands and hair drifting in the dim, weightless atmosphere, her eyeballs darting behind her thin lids in dream.

"I'm opening the door now," he says, and I can see the smoke glowing at the end of the hall where light from Nadine's bedroom illuminates the cloud.

"Shame you got weasels," he says, closing the door. "Once you get'em you pretty much got'em for good." From far away I hear the sound of the capsule being sealed by technicians, and the gantry slowly pulling away.

✦ Potter's Field

Lawrence was watching Mrs. Travis through his telescope as she moved through the dim light of the morning. Dressed in gray and blue, she carried a silver platter through her backyard and into a long shed. On the platter was French toast. Forty-eight servings. Lawrence's window was down so he couldn't hear the noise. Usually they kicked up a storm when Mrs. Travis fed them. They pounded on the bars of their cages in rapture and hollered.

"Are you up? Lawrence? Are you?"

Lawrence associated his grandmother's voice with the gruntings of wild hogs or hippopotami.

"I'm up."

The Travis's backyard was now without motion or sound. Lawrence aimed the telescope out toward the ocean, toward the gray shore of Hart Island.

Nudd appeared in the door. "Why don't you answer me?"

Lawrence turned toward her. He was wearing his Department of Correction uniform. On his chin was a small cut from his father's straight razor.

"Well?"

He looked at Nudd with a vast loathing and disgust. "I did."

"Oh." His grandmother looked at Lawrence adoringly. "Look at you," she said, beaming at his uniform. She spread her arms open and approached him with the slow, impending speed of an asteroid. Lawrence smelled vodka.

"Morning time is love time," Nudd said.

Lawrence's eyes bulged in their sockets as she squeezed him. When she at last let go, he turned his back and took a final look through the telescope. He could feel his grandmother staring at the back of his head. All was quiet next door. A bell on a buoy swung out in the Sound; a tug pulled a long flatboat toward Hellgate.

"You be on your best behavior today," Nudd said. "You have to kiss a little ass, you kiss a little ass. That won't kill you."

"No, ma'am," Lawrence said.

Nudd beamed. "You are spoiled rotten," she said. "I'm not kidding. Spoiled rotten."

Looking into the telescope, squinting with one eye, Lawrence made his Death Face.

When he got downstairs, he found a half-grapefruit waiting for him on the kitchen table. The sun streamed onto a red-and-white checkered tablecloth. Nudd had placed a cherry in the middle of the grapefruit; judging from the smell, she had poured a jigger of brandy on it as well.

"I have to run," Lawrence said.

"You do what you have to do," Nudd said. "Don't even think about the trouble I went through to make you a nice breakfast."

"Okay," Lawrence said. "I won't."

Lawrence started moving toward the door. Before he reached it, he knew that she would call his name, preventing his escape. Her voice was all the more horrible when he could predict what it would say.

"Lawrence . . . "

"Yes, Nudd."

"I'm making chicken à la king tonight."

"Great. I have to go. Really. I'm late."

"You are spoiled rotten," Nudd said. "Absolutely rotten."

Mrs. Travis, wearing a satin bathrobe, was picking the paper up off her driveway as Lawrence walked by the monkey orphanage. "Good morning," Lawrence said.

"Ah, what's so good about it?"

Lawrence rolled his eyes, felt like giving her a piece of his mind. "It's just an expression," he said, bitterly.

Mrs. Travis sighed. "Oh, Lawrence, what's wrong with me? It's not your fault."

"What's not my fault?"

"Anything."

"Is everything all right, Mrs. Travis?"

"Ah, Lawrence. You see how it is. Our Sue-Sue died last night."

"Oh," Lawrence said. "I'm sorry."

Down by the dock a whistle blew.

"She was my favorite," Mrs. Travis said. "We had her twelve years."

"I really am sorry."

"We got her from a psychiatrist. Sue-Sue belonged to his son. When he got divorced, the wife got custody of the son and the psychiatrist got custody of Sue-Sue. He slit his throat. The monkey lived but the psychiatrist went insane." Mrs. Travis turned her back, shaking her head."Crazy world."

Lawrence watched Mrs. Travis recede. The sign marked Simian Refuge Center swung in the breeze, next to a large brass bell. A unicycle lay on its side in the front yard.

Again the boat moaned. Swearing to himself, Lawrence ran down Fordham Street. As he came over the hill, passing through the long shadow of the Methodists' steeple, he could see the morgue ferry sailing out to sea. The tin stack puffed blue smoke. Lawrence reached the end of the dock, watched the ferry disappear.

"Goddammit to hell."

A wooden shack bore the sign: Department of Correction: Keep Out. A single light bulb dangled down on a wire. No one was home.

As a child, he had stood here with his mother, waiting for his father to sail the morgue ferry up to the dock. He had seemed like royalty to Lawrence then, waving to them from behind the wheel of the enormous boat.

Lawrence did not remember how old he was when he first learned what his father did for a living. The telescope had come to him on his ninth or tenth birthday, the same year he got the boomerang. One of the first things the telescope had shown him was the sight of the distant convicts on Hart, dressed in green, unloading the caskets of the homeless off of his father's ferry. Later he went out to throw the boomerang, but there was something wrong with it. The boomerang soared out above the ocean and did not come back.

He turned his back and looked toward the land. Broken boats were stacked up on cinder blocks, their hulls green and gray from the ocean. Water lapped on the rocks; a seagull slept on a sailboat mast.

Lawrence eyed the dead boats, where his father had said the ghost of Louisa van Slyke lived. She was the first person to have been buried in the potter's field on Hart Island. She had died in May 1865, and was listed in the records of the New York City morgue as being "twenty-four and friendless." Louisa van Slyke's ghost was supposed to walk abroad in May, committing the kinds of crimes traceable to a lack of friendship.

Lawrence's grandmother was speaking idly of getting one of her friends to move in with them. The neighborhood was changing; the Shefflers' house had been ransacked while the Shefflers slept upstairs. A television and a typewriter had been stolen. A week later Lawrence's house had been broken into while he and his grandmother were out buying pillow stuffing. The vandals had broken a window in the room that had once belonged to Lawrence's father and had stolen several items from the room, including a ten-gallon hat, a small blue megaphone from college days, and a pennant marked: Yale.

"Hey, you. You the new kid?"

"Yes, sir."

"You're late."

"Yes, sir."

"They left without you."

"Is there any way of getting over to the island now?"

"Yeah. Lucky for you. I'm going over in the skiff. My name's Stoddard."

"Pleased to meet you, sir." Lawrence walked down a long ramp to a small floating dock.

"Climb aboard." Lawrence stepped into the motorboat. He positioned himself near the stern.

"All right," said Stoddard. "I hope you don't mind getting wet."

"No, sir."

"Cut the sir crap," Stoddard said. "Everybody calls me Jack." The outboard started, and they began to skid across the Sound. As City Island receded, Lawrence saw his house, the monkey orphanage, the Methodist church, all growing small.

Stoddard yelled something over the whine of the outboard.

"What?"

"I said, 'So you're Monahan's boy.' "

"Yes. I am."

"A good man, your father. We all respected him; we respected the hell out of him." A big wave splashed over the gunwale. "I'm real sorry about what happened. You ever want to talk sometime, you just let me know. Always ready to listen." Another wave rocked them. "Of course, I hope you're not expecting special treatment. You might as well know you're starting at the bottom of the bottom."

"I know, sir."

"Jack," Stoddard said. "Everybody calls me Jack."

"Jack."

"Yes, sir, the bottom of the bottom," Stoddard laughed. "But what the hell. That won't kill you."

Stoddard drew the skiff up to a long wooden dock and cut the engine. The boat drifted toward a piling, and Stoddard jumped onto the dock.

He showed Lawrence the knot to use when mooring a boat. Lawrence said he understood. Stoddard clapped him on the back and led him up a gravel path leading toward a small hill. To the left of the hill was a bowl-shaped meadow with a single cypress on the rim.

"That's the Vale," Stoddard said. He sounded as if he wanted to say more. "Your daddy ever tell you much about what goes on out here, Monahan?"

"No, sir. Not much, that is."

"Ah, well. That's all right. Sure it is."

At the top of the hill were a flagpole and several mobile homes. Stoddard led Lawrence up a small set of wooden stairs in front of one of the trailers. "I think the captain is expecting you." He patted him on the back. "Don't worry, son," he said. "He's just like anyone else."

Captain Webb sat behind a large desk in a wood-paneled room. He was drinking coffee from a styrofoam cup. "Captain," said Stoddard. A glass jar of jellybeans stood next to a small clipboard.

"Stoddard," Webb said, squinting. "And you're Monahan's boy."

"Yes, sir."

There was a growling sound from the corner; next to the desk stood the most pitiful dog Lawrence had ever seen. It seemed to be part pit bull and part orang-utan; as Lawrence entered the room, the dog stood up. It had three legs. A moving chain of drool hung from its jowls, dripping into a puddle on the floor.

"You're late."

"Yes, sir."

"Why?"

"I missed the boat."

"You missed the boat." Webb took a jellybean from the jar, held it between his thumb and his index finger. "You know what happens to men who miss the boat, Monahan?"

The dog sat down and licked itself.

"No, sir."

Webb squeezed the jellybean until it oozed between his finger and his thumb.

"That's what."

"Yes, sir."

There was a knock. The dog barked.

"Dammit!" Webb raised his hand as if to strike the dog. "Shut up, Lars. Ah. Calcagno. At last."

A short man with large jowls stepped into the room. His bloodshot eyes shifted from Webb to Lawrence, then back again. He sniffed.

"Calcagno, Monahan. Monahan, Calcagno. Calcagno here is going to be showing you around. Isn't that right, Calcagno?"

"You're the boss man."

"Fine. Show him the ropes, then start him to work doing something."

"Such as what?"

"I don't know. Whatever needs doing."

Lawrence understood. He was now the only person on the entire island lower than Calcagno. Lawrence's arrival was moving Calcagno up a notch. This was Calcagno's big day.

"See you later, Chief."

"You keep an eye on this Monahan, now, hear?"

Calcagno led Lawrence out a side door, escorted him toward a large field. In the midst was an idle backhoe, a pile of dirt, and a group of men in uniforms. There were prisoners in a hole shoveling dirt onto the pile.

"God, I hate him," Calcagno said, feeling his nose. "I mean he is just like a total robot head." Calcagno looked around fearfully. "We better keep our voices down, man. There's always somebody listening."

One of the guards cast a glance toward them. "So listen," Calcagno said. "Right here you got your digger-uppers, man. A bad job. You get one or two of these a week. This field here used to be all grown over, but we got it all fixed up now, man. Looks nice, huh?"

"What do you mean, digger-uppers?"

Calcagno laughed out of one side of his mouth. "Zackly what it sounds like, man. Somebody somewhere finally figures out who somebody is, and we have to ship them back."

"But . . . how do you know who's who?"

"Well you gotta keep records, man. We put numbers on the boxes. There's a list with the names on it. You'll be in charge of that, man. I'll show you Records later."

Calcagno started to lead Lawrence down the hill.

"Why do people want to dig them up again?"

"All kinds of reasons. You want your relatives buried here?"

"Well . . . no."

"Sometimes it's the government, man. Somebody turns out to have been a big shot in the army, they move'em to Arlington. Other times, a family finds out after they're buried. You know. We've had some real hoi polloi buried out here, man. Once they get identified, the families want them back. We had that kid, the one that was in the Walt Disney movies when he was small. Johnny something? I don't know. What is it? Like I can't believe I can't remember his name. Jay North? No that was Dennis the Menace, man. Damn. Anyway, you should have seen it. Boy oh boy, what a mess that was. Right after the rains. That's the worst time, right after the rains, man, cause all the water seeps down into the boxes. And the one you want is always on the bottom. It's not a pretty story, man."

They were walking on a gravel path past some rosebushes. Out on the sea a tug was hauling a tanker covered with valves and pipes and ladders.

"What do you mean, they were on the bottom?"

"You'll see how we bury'em when we get over to the field, man. Six down and two across. What I mean is usually the one you want is the sixth one down. Anyway, first I'm going to show you the old village. The path we're on leads straight around, man. You see that marker?"

On a flat field stood a single monument. Beyond it loomed some ruined buildings.

"That's the only tombstone on the place. One size fits all, you know what I mean? Huh-huh-huh."

"What does it say on the marker?"

"Now there you got me . . . it's something from the Bible. It's nice. I read it once. Soothing. Peaceful. Here's the old prison."

They stood in the shadow of a large stone building. There were square holes where the windows had been. The roof was missing. Pigeons cooed and rustled on a Victorian-style porch.

"Used to be a hotel, man. About a hundred years ago. Then a prison. Once the city bought the island. Then they turned it into a loony bin, man. That closed."

Calcagno opened his mouth and laughed with one half of it.

"Come on, I'll show you the rest of the village."

They walked down a long street bordered by shuttered shop windows and closed-up buildings. In one store a sign swung on a hinge: Butcher's.

"Everything's pretty much the way it was a hundred years ago. Except destroyed, man."

"How come everything's in such bad condition?"

"Vandals, man." Calcagno sounded irritated. "Say, Monahan, you ever have a job before?"

"What do you mean?"

"Well, I don't know. You have to be sharp on this job."

"All right, I'm sharp."

"Good. Now take me. I'm pretty sharp. I didn't use to be, but I am now." Calcagno smiled. "I'm as sharp as a button."

Lawrence opened his mouth, then shut it again. He thought momentarily of hitting Calcagno on the head with something and trying to swim back home.

"How do the vandals get here?" Lawrence asked. "I mean, there's pretty tight security, from what I've seen."

"Well, of course there's tight security. It's a prison, man. I mean we only have like twenty prisoners out here at a time, man. Just enough to bury the boxes they send us up. The vandals don't come now, they came in the past. Before we started fixing up the place. But they used to come out in boats. From the Bronx. They'd get in rowboats with like spray paint, man, and like cherry bombs, man, and like dynamite, and they'd come over here and just wail on the place. There's a couple buildings that don't even exist anymore. I'll show you those later."

"What's this?"

"That's the old mess hall, man. Not in bad condition. I mean there's still a roof and everything. But I wouldn't go in there now. There's rats the size of Orson Welles, man."

"I don't want to go in."

"I mean you'll have to go in sometime, man. That's part of the job. Going in places like that." Calcagno licked his lips. "I had to go in there. I didn't like it at first. Now I don't mind so much. The trick is to make a lot of noise so the rats know you're coming. Usually they'll go and do something else."

Lawrence looked up the street, where there were boarded-up mansions with rotting front porches.

"You see these houses, man? People used to live here. Before the city bought the island. It was like a resort. The people are gone now, but their houses are still here. There's nothing in 'em though. I've checked. A little furniture. Some pants."

They stood before a small church. There were holes in the roof.

"Church, man," Calcagno said. "The pipe organ's still in there. You gotta be careful, though. Chunks of the ceiling can fall on your head, man. I once got hit by a pretty big one, but I'm okay."

They turned around and looked at the deserted street. Lawrence imagined the doors of the butcher shop swinging open, people walking in and out of the old houses.

Calcagno rubbed his teeth with his forefinger.

"So. That's the old village, man. Let's walk over to the burial site, then I'll show you Records, then I'll get you to work. You mind working outside?"

"No."

"I'll put you on the tractor. Gotta spread some fertilizer, man."

At the bottom of a small meadow was a metal dock and a steel rowboat. A sign above the dock read: For Emergency Use Only.

"Oh, I almost forgot. This place we're walking over right now, man, this is called the Vale. This is where all the amputated arms and limbs from the city hospitals go, man."

"You're not serious."

"You think I'm not serious? You're the one who's going to have to keep track of them, man."

"But it doesn't make any sense. They really bury them? What's the point?"

"Well," Calcagno said, shaking his head, "they can't just throw them away, can they? I mean, that's kind of barbaric, don't you think?"

"But . . . burying them . . . out here . . . on an island in the middle of the Sound . . . "

"Hey, I didn't make the rules," Calcagno said.

"I didn't say you made the rules."

"Don't get mad, Monahan. Sometimes people will have the arms and legs buried wherever they expect the rest of them to be buried. When they die, I mean. If they already have a plot. But if they don't they get sent out here."

Calcagno took a banana out of his back pocket and began to peel it.

"All right, all right," Lawrence said, walking more quickly. "I take your word for it."

"You're kind of squeamish, aren't you, Monahan?"

"What? No. Don't say that."

Banana smell entered Lawrence's nostrils. "Listen," Calcagno said, chewing. "It's just, you know, working out here takes a certain blindness sometimes, you know what I mean? You have to learn not to think. I know I don't. I mean, like, sure, some days I'll be using the forklift taking the boxes off the ferry, man, and I'll think, well damn, someone's body is inside this thing. But usually I just load'em up and take'em down to the site, man. You have to keep your eyes closed, Monahan. That won't kill you."

They were approaching a small field in which a Department of

Correction van was parked. Several guards stood around a hole. There were a dozen men in the pit, wearing green. In the back of the van were a dozen pine coffins. Lawrence stopped walking and looked at the field. The guards had guns trained on the prisoners.

Calcagno threw the peel on the ground and smiled, pushing mush between his teeth. "Hey, Monahan," he said. "You sure this isn't your first job?"

It was late in the afternoon and Lawrence was sitting behind the wheel of a small tractor. The tractor hauled a small fertilizer spreader with a rope. He was fertilizing the field that held the single marker. "They usually get prisoners to do this," Calcagno had said. "But there's a shortage."

The marker said:

I am the Alpha and the Omega
The beginning and the end
Weep not for us
For we are with the father
No longer do we cast shadows on the ground
As you do
We are at peace

Lawrence was driving around and around in a circle. He was wondering how he could ever have agreed to take a job as pitiful and stupid as this. "You have to work to eat," his grandmother had said. "You have to eat to live." The tractor made a low whining sound, like the drone of a squadron of airplanes. Every now and then the tractor would strike one of the small concrete markers imprinted with identification numbers. Plot 17, Section 85A. Sometimes the markers would knock against the spreader, and it would ring with a hollow sound like a deep, broken bell.

In April the Travises had had a funeral for one of the monkeys. They had a small casket made, and Lucy had lain in state in the Travises' backyard. Lucy was the first monkey they got. It had belonged to a relative. When Mrs. Travis first brought Lucy over to the Monahans' house, Lawrence's grandmother had said, "Why don't you just take it to the zoo?"

Mrs. Travis had looked flabbergasted. "Zoos? Do you know what goes on in a zoo? Do you know what happens to new monkeys in a zoo? They get beaten. Starve. They die. You might as well kill them yourself."

For a while Lucy had lived in a cage in the kitchen. Later on Mr. Travis had built the monkey house out back. They lived in cages, one atop the other. When you opened the front door of the shed, you saw row after row of folded hands resting on the bars. Mrs. Travis warned Lawrence not to go into the monkey house by himself. They could reach out when you weren't looking and bite your fingers off.

Lawrence drove around and around Plot 17, moving clockwise. The spreader banged and bumped against the concrete markers. The tractor droned.

Lawrence's eyes lost focus as he felt sorrier and sorrier for himself. This is, without question, the worst of all imaginable ways to spend one's life, he thought. You'd think they'd give me a break after everything I've been through. You would think. But no: they've left me completely alone: orphaned, shipwrecked. Stuck out here spreading fertilizer. While Calcagno is off torturing chipmunks someplace. Stupid, pitiful, idiotic, son-of-a-bitch Calcagno.

A small black shadow stood watching Lawrence. It was Webb's dog, Lars. The dog was standing on its three legs, frozen, its tail erect. It was pointing at Lawrence.

He remembered Mrs. Travis's face in the morning, when, standing in her bathrobe, she had told him Sue-Sue had died. Things were not going well for the Travises. They owned a chimpanzee named Marbles that had escaped about a month earlier. It had not returned and was presumed to have starved to death, or to have been run over by a car. The Travises did not like Marbles, since a chimpanzee turned out to be more work than the monkeys. About the only thing it could do was ride a unicycle.

I live the strangest life in the world, Lawrence thought. No one would believe how incredible, how incomprehensibly stupid, how essentially pitiful my life is. It's a miracle, if you think about it. He shuddered.

The sun disappeared behind the central monument, which loomed suddenly in front of him. The tractor's left front wheel struck the marble; the tractor groaned, and the engine went dead. There was barking. The monument swayed, then tipped and collapsed backward. There was a sickening, snapping sound, then silence. The epitaph on the monument faced the sky.

Lawrence looked around to see if anyone had noticed what had happened, but he was alone. The silence was strange after hearing the engine drone for so long. Lawrence's ears rang. The sound of bells on the buoys came to him from far away.

The dog was not quite dead. The tail and part of the hindquarters protruded from beneath the fallen monument. The tail quivered slightly. Lawrence was not sure what he should do. He tried tugging on the monument, but he could not move it. The dog's tail trembled then lay still.

A small part of the monument had broken off from the rest. It had the word "No" engraved on it. The only thing to do now was to try to get the dog out from under the monument, and to hide it somewhere. Then he could just blame the falling of the monument on the wind. It certainly wasn't his fault it had been so shoddily attached to the pedestal. Why should he have to feel guilty about what wasn't even his fault?

Lawrence wedged the chip with the word "No" on it between the earth and the monument. He disengaged the spreader and wrapped the rope around the dog's belly. He used the knot that Stoddard had taught him. He turned the tractor around, gave it a little gas. The dog's carcass slowly edged out from beneath the tomb.

Lawrence cut the motor. The bells on the Sound seemed louder now. The guards would soon be coming to see what was wrong with the tractor; everyone could hear that something was wrong. They had said they were going to keep a close watch on him.

Lawrence picked up the dog and walked quickly toward the old prison.

"Hey," a voice said. "Monahan. What are you doing?"

Lawrence didn't look back to see who was calling. In his arms, the dog was warm and light.

The old village was bathed in long shadows now, the sun disappearing behind the ruined prison. Lawrence ran down the main street, past the butcher's and the mess hall and the old houses. He approached the ruined chapel. In the distance people were calling his name.

The interior of the chapel was dark, except for two spotlights thrown on the floor by holes in the roof. The outlines of a ruined pipe organ were visible above the altar. Lawrence put the dog down in one of the pools of light, then sat down in a pew. His arms felt light; he wanted to raise them over his head and stretch his fingers open so that they would look like starfish.

They were getting closer now. Their voices were echoing down the long deserted streets of the old village.

Lawrence looked toward the open sections of the ceiling overhead and remembered what Calcagno had said about it falling on him. That's all I want, Lawrence thought, is the roof to fall on me. A sign.

He stared at the ceiling, listening to the guards come closer.

Lawrence left Lars in the church and ran down the street toward the mess hall. It was hard to tell where the guards were; the buildings bounced the voices in every direction. In front of him was a picket fence surrounding the graves of Union army soldiers.

"Monahan!"

He ran into one of the abandoned houses. He was in a rotting parlor; a dilapidated staircase led to a second floor. Lawrence creaked up the stairs.

The house was filled with peeling wallpaper, fallen plaster, a few random articles of furniture. Lawrence opened the door to what must have been the master bedroom. Two bay windows, glass intact, looked out over the Sound. An oil tanker, miles and miles long, lurched toward Hellgate. Small pleasure craft were leaning into the wind.

On the floor was random detritus: a copper pipe, a pair of shoes, an empty bottle of wine. Lawrence picked up the copper pipe, feeling its smooth, cool surface in his hand. He looked out the window: he could make out the outline of the steeple of the Methodist church on Fordham Street; he could see the long Department of Correction dock jutting out into the water from City Island.

He wanted to hold the pipe to his eyes and look as if through a telescope upon the broad expanse of the Sound. This room must have been the room of a sailor, Lawrence thought. Someone who stood just as he was standing, looking out on the ocean. He watched the sun disappear behind the steeple and felt cold. The old house was growing dark now, and no one was calling him.

Lawrence went back downstairs, and walked through the streets of the old village. He passed by a low-built structure that bore the sign: Dynamo Room. In an open doorway were dozens of frozen gears, rusted turbines. Lawrence kept on walking until he arrived at the ocean. He walked on the beach in front of the Vale, down to the small metal pier and the steel rowboat and the sign that said: For Emergency Use Only.

It was a lot more difficult than Lawrence expected. The oars kept coming out of the oarlocks, and, because he wasn't facing the direction in which he was moving, he had to keep stopping and twisting around in his seat. By that time the current would turn the boat in the wrong direction, and he would have to spend several minutes rowing with one oar in order to re-orient himself. At one point a huge tanker loomed out of the night, narrowly missing him. It blew a deep, long blast. The tanker was so close he could see the rivets on the hull and the individual drops of water on the portholes. He bounced up and down in the tanker's wake.

He beached the boat in front of the cemetery of the Methodist church. He placed the oars in the boat: they made a hollow clunk. They would find the boat tomorrow. Tomorrow they would come after him and make him explain everything. Tomorrow his grandmother would cry; tomorrow they would fire him and say he was a disgrace to his family's name. Tomorrow all these terrible things would happen to him, but he no longer cared. Tonight he wanted only peace and quiet, his own room, a door with a lock that locked.

He walked up through the graveyard, his clothes wet, his shoes heavy, then stopped, listening. A sound came from the churchyard, a low rumbling as if the headstones were being withdrawn into the ground. At the top of the hill flickered a dancing shadow—something moving chaotically, joyously, with no sense of balance or equilibrium. The figure threw back its head and screamed a long, rapturous laugh into the night, as it balanced precariously on the unicycle, wearing a ten-gallon hat and carrying a small blue megaphone and a pennant that said: Yale.

✦ Lost in Space

"Dad told Will and me never to touch the laser guns without permission."—Penny Robinson

✦ ✦ ✦

Twice a year I tune the piano of a tiny man who lives on the third floor of an abandoned home in Centralia, Pennsylvania, the site of the Centralia mine disaster. Steam from the underground fire pours from boreholes in a scythed cornfield. As raindrops hit the ground made hot by the mine fire, they hiss softly, evaporating in a small cloud, like thin gray exhaust from a five-and-dime cap gun.

✦ ✦ ✦

Astronaut Pete Conrad (Apollo 12): You know what I feel like, Al?
Astronaut Alan Bean: What?
Conrad: Did you ever see those pictures with giraffes running in slow motion?

✦ ✦ ✦

I knock the fork against my knee, listen. My foot swings forward. Reflexes.

"Hey, take a load off of it already," Mr. Taconnelli says. "Here. Let me take your shoes."

"No, I'm all right." I'm trying to hear the pitch.

"Please. Give me your shoes. You'll insult me if you don't."

I sit down on a stool and take off my blue boots.

"Thank you," he says, taking them from me, and tosses them into the corner. Too late I see a pile of hundreds of pairs of shoes reaching all the way from Taconnelli's decaying bedroom up to heaven.

✦ ✦ ✦

Astronaut Harrison Schmitt (Apollo 17): Oh, hey! There is orange soil!
Astronaut Eugene Cernan: Well, don't move it till I see it.
Schmitt: I stirred it up with my feet.

63

Cernan: Hey, here it is. I can see it from here.

Schmitt: It's orange.

Cernan: Wait a minute. Let me put my visor up. [*pause*] It's still orange.

Schmitt: Sure is! Crazy! Orange!

Cernan: I've got to dig a trench, Houston.

Houston: Copy that. I guess we'd better work fast.

Schmitt: He's not going out of his wits. It really is orange. It's almost the same color as the LMP decal on my camera.

Cernan: That is orange, Jack.

✦   ✦   ✦

"I'll have'em back to you in a couple days," Mr. Taconnelli says, disregarding my shoes. I'm working on middle C. "I got a lot of orders backed up. I swear when you get them back you won't know them. You'll swear they're someone else's."

He puts the barbells down, goes over to the open window. Across the street are the ruins of something called Christmas Village. Reins trail from Santa's hands toward the antlered remains of eight metal skeletons. Comet and Vixen, torsoless, hang suspended in midflight.

✦   ✦   ✦

Conrad: Another interesting thing is this white or gray-white moon in contrast, very startling, with the black sky, just like everyone has reported. The black is about as black as you've ever seen in your life. The moon just sort of very light, concrete color. In fact, if I wanted to look at something that I thought was the same color as the moon, I'd go out and look at my driveway.

[*static*]

We're passing over the Sea of Fertility now and it's a little darker than the terrain that we've been over, but not much—more a slightly darker gray. Looks like the beach sand, down at Galveston. Whenever it's wet.

✦   ✦   ✦

"Hey, Hey, you. Look at this." Taconnelli pulls a photo album off of a bookcase and hands it to me. "That's me," he says, indicating the small man standing next to the circus cannon. RUDOLPH TACONNELLI, the sign next to the cannon says. THE HUMAN CANNONBALL.

"Oh," I say. "You were in the circus."

"Boulton Brothers," he says. "Thirty-two and one-half years. Best years of my life. If only we had a cannon around this place I'd show you some real fun."

✦   ✦   ✦

Vice-President George Bush: There's been a serious incident with the space shuttle, sir.
National Security Affairs Advisor John Poindexter: A major malfunction.
Director of Communications Pat Buchanan: Sir, the shuttle has exploded.
[President Ronald Reagan stands up]
President Reagan: How tragic. *[pause]* Is that the one the schoolteacher was on?

✦   ✦   ✦

"Nah," I say. "It sounds too dangerous to be fun."

"You don't know anything," Taconnelli says. "You've got to use your head. First of all, imagine the crowd. Tent all filled with people, all of 'em spread out like dandelions in the field. There's peanut guys up in the stands, a band somewhere. Elephants blowing off their trunks, clowns in the corners. The ringmaster introduces you, points across the ring toward the biggest goddamned cannon you've ever seen. You're standing there in sequins, silver, blue, the color of the sun on the sea, my boy, or the roof of a barn at twilight, summertime. They lift you up; everything is disappearing as you slide down the nozzle. You've only got the one spotlight from the mouth of the cannon letting light down on you. They tilt it up, the drums are rolling. Maybe a baby crying somewhere in the back. You're in the tube, making yourself real small, making yourself into something like a little globe, you're in there. You're waiting for the charge. Up the long tunnel, a spotlight pointing toward the top of the tent comes down, maybe you can see the high wire, way overhead. One of the Flying Whatdoyoucallems waves with a small blue glove. You're in there thinking, floating in an lightless ocean of hard-boiled egg yolks, consumed by the smell of sulfur."

✦   ✦   ✦

"Dr. Smith, when will you stop acting so silly?"—Penny Robinson

✦   ✦   ✦

I'm working on the bass strings, two octaves below middle C. Taconnelli is gesturing with his hands. "When the explosion hits you, it hits you from underneath, almost from inside. Everything turns into a blur of love, fire, antigravity. Your pants are smoking, leaving a little jet trail. If you move right you can make skywriting. You reach that perfect midpoint of the flight, Johnson, when you've gone as high as you're going to go, but, before you come back down, you're held right there in the air, looking down on all the faces looking up. Clowns are scurrying below you, trying to get the fire engines out of the way. Elephants look like galoshes. In a second you'll start to fall but for that moment you're free from gravity, free from it all. Infinity, my boy! Your pants are still smoking. You see some pretty thing on the ground, maybe one of the dancing girls, you see one of the Boulton Brothers counting money in his wallet. Sometimes the back of your haircut brushes against the canvas overhead. You see the first-aid truck in the corner, and then—down you go, falling, falling, forgetting your name until the net catches you, bounces you up and down a few times. You stand to your feet and raise your arms up in the air, your hands feel small. And the crowd goes wild.

"That's what it's like to be a human cannonball, Johnson. Jesus, if we had a cannon around this place I'd show you exactly what I mean."

✦ ✦ ✦

Astronaut David Scott (Apollo 15): Oh my. It is green. It is green.
Astronaut James Irwin: I told you. It's green.
Scott: Fantastic. This has got to be something. And it looks . . . hey, now
  it's gray! The visor makes it green, Jim!

✦ ✦ ✦

"You make it sound easy. I don't know if I believe in that."

"Well, it is easy. Once you're flying through the air, anyway. Any moron can do that. But taking off, that's the hard part. You have to make yourself awfully round to keep from being blown up. We *are* talking about gunpowder here, you know. TNT! Nitroglycerine! This isn't the kind of job for anybody, at least not until they blow you up."

"Why'd you give it up, you like it so much."

"Ah . . . " Taconnelli stands at the window again, takes back the album. "I had an accident, a close call. Missed the net one time, gave me a little scare. Landed on the thin man. I had a boy about your age— Vincent—if you'd clean yourself up you'd look like him almost. Of course that'll be the day. Vinnie took over the act after I overshot the net that time, I figured it was time for him to make something of himself anyway. Ah, if you could have seen his face the first time we blew him up. When he came down, I could tell it was in his blood. I started a new act for myself, something for my declining years you understand, Taconnelli the Human Bomb. Kind of like what I'd done before, except without the cannon. I wouldn't blow myself up, of course, I mean not completely. I'm not stupid."

✦ ✦ ✦

Flight Supervisor, Alpha Control: "Message to the president, on scramble. [*pause*] Sir, the *Jupiter 2* is moving at incredible speeds, beyond the edges of our galaxy. I'm afraid . . . that from this moment onward . . . the Robinson family is presumed to be . . . hopelessly . . . lost in space."

✦ ✦ ✦

I'm still working on the bass notes. The second A below middle C is too close to the harp so I'm going to have to put in a tuner's knot. Taconnelli is pacing. "You take my advice, you play it safe, Johnson. I mean, let me shoot you through a cannon, if I can find one, but after that, I mean, play it safe. You only get one life and that's the truth."

He wipes his forehead. "I can still see Vinnie getting into the cannon. He always had to outdo me in everything. Had to prove he was better than his old man. He had them point the cannon straight up, I mean straight up into the sky. The drums rolled, the elephants yelled. They shot him off, and up he went, over our heads, past the high wire, burst right through the canvas of the big top. Made a big hole, too, let in the starlight. We all just stood there, watching, waiting, but he didn't come back down. I went outside but there was nothing. I thought I saw a star go in and out, like maybe he was passing by one, but I think it was just the atmosphere. You know how blobs in the air make the stars twinkle? One of those. I went back inside, didn't know what to do. People were clapping. The show went on. Fat lady sat on a teeny-weeny stool. The Small Man sang a song, Hans Gunter-Hildegarde whipped some lions in a cage. About an hour and a half later, after two intermissions, Vinnie came back down, came straight through the hole in the big top he'd made the first time, plummeted down into the nozzle of the cannon we'd shot him out of. People didn't know what to do, so they started applauding. Suddenly Vinnie appears out of the top of the cannon, and waves. His pants are smoking, but he's okay. Tears came out of my eyes. I waved to him. I started yelling, 'I love you, son. I love you.' He was crying, too, although that might have been because his clothes were on fire. He's yelling 'I love you dad.' The Fat Lady held me in her arms, which was kind of like sitting in a huge chair, and we were all crying, smiling, laughing, yelling. It was like V-E Day. It was New Year's Eve in Times Square. The audience is tearing out its hair.

"They started this chant. At first I didn't understand it, but at last the words took form. They were yelling: 'Shoot him off again! Shoot him off again!'

"Vinnie waved. We got some more fuse. Vinnie disappeared. When we blew him off again, people were silent. They just watched him soar straight up, as if gravity for him had been called off.

"Well, it was late, and people really wanted to see him blown up a lot more than they wanted to see him come back, kind of like the Crucifixion, and so the crowd thinned out and went home. I went back to my tent, got out of costume. A couple of hours went by, and still he hadn't come back. An airplane went by overhead, there was a distant ping like a BB hitting the edge of a cymbal a mile away. Boulton came by, told me my boy had done good, said he'd get a raise. He clapped me on the back, it was awful, I should have known. The Monkey Boy came by, we gave him some hot dogs. Then, a streak of light, a small comet. Vinnie comes soaring down, landing on the Monkey Boy. The hot dog goes flying.

"See, what had happened was, was, Vinnie had hit his head on the underbelly of that airplane. That's what the sound was. He was dead before he even got back into the gravity again, even before he started falling that big fall back to earth."

✦   ✦   ✦

Scott: Oh, look at the mountains [of the moon] today, Jim. When they're all sunlit. Isn't that beautiful?
Irwin: Dave, I'm reminded about my favorite biblical passage from Psalms. "I'll look unto the hills from whence cometh my help."

✦   ✦   ✦

I'm working on the upper octaves now. That tuner's knot is going to cost Taconnelli an extra fifteen bucks. He doesn't know that yet. "Well, the show must go on, you know, so the next night I had to do the Human Bomb all by myself. I didn't feel like going back to the cannon. I swallowed about forty pounds of nitroglycerine. It's not bad once you get used to it. It was only when I lay on my back, ready to touch myself off, that I changed my mind. I looked up at the hole in the tent, saw the stars, realized Vinnie wouldn't like it if I blew myself up. Life is better than death, you know. If that wasn't true, do you think I'd even bother getting the piano tuned? What do I look like to you, an idiot? No, you have to believe in things. You don't want to be dead if you can avoid it.

"So. I quit, came down here, live on the money the government sends. It's not a bad life, although it was better before Christmas Village burned down. View's kind of depressing now. Santa's Castle all smoldery, it's sad."

I clap him on the back. "Don't worry, old man. Maybe we'll find you a cannon someplace. You can blow me up."

✦ ✦ ✦

Astronaut Buzz Aldrin (Apollo 11): The blue color of my boot has completely disappeared now into this—still don't know what color to describe this other than grayish cocoa color. It appears to be covering most of the lighter part of my boot . . . very fine particles . . .

Astronaut Neil Armstrong: It's kind of falling all over me while I'm doing this.

Aldrin: Kind of like soot, huh?

Armstrong: It looks like [*static*] down here.

Aldrin: I think my watch stopped Neil. [*pause*] No, it didn't either. [*pause*] Second hand.

✦ ✦ ✦

Taconnelli does not like being slapped on the back. "Careful!" he shouts, recoiling from my touch. "Good God, man, watch out. You have to be gentle. You don't know who you're dealing with."

"Sure I do," I say. I'm pulling out the tuning felts now. "You're the Human Cannonball, right?"

"You don't understand. See, you have to be gentle. The nitroglycerine. It's still inside, see?"

"Oh, come on," I say. "Surely you've digested it by now."

"Johnson," he says. "It stays with you."

✦ ✦ ✦

Aldrin: As I look around the area, the contrast in general is . . .
[*static*] . . . looking down sun, zero phase, it's a very light-colored
gray, light gray color. I see a halo around my own shadow, around the
shadow of my helmet.

✦ ✦ ✦

Taconnelli hands me a twenty.

"It's thirty-five," I say. "Fifteen extra for the tuner's knot."

He mutters to himself, digs around in his pockets. "You got any kids,
Johnson?" he says.

"Kids? Me? No." He hands me the money.

"One thing about the circus. You get kind of tired of kids."

I'm putting the wrenches and the tuning fork back in the toolbox.
Taconnelli is back at the window again, looking at the smoke.

"Except your own. Goddammit. If everything was different, then
we'd be talking. Poor Vinnie. If I had a cannon big enough I'd shoot
everyone I know through the hole in the top of the tent. There'd just be
the two of us. Without all these other bastards underfoot all the time.
It would be like heaven down here."

✦ ✦ ✦

Astronaut Judith Resnik (*Challenger*): I think something is only dangerous if you are not prepared for it. Or if you don't have enough control
over it or if you can't think through how to get yourself out of a problem.
[Judith Resnik was a gourmet cook and a classical pianist.] I never play
anything softly.

✦ ✦ ✦

"Play me something," Taconnelli says. "Play me a song before you go.
Something sad and loud so I can sing along. I love to sing. It's as much
fun as yelling, only nobody gets mad. Play me something like that."

Self-consciously at first, then with more confidence, I play part of
Pictures at an Exhibition. There are no lyrics to *With the Dead in a Dead
Language,* but Taconnelli is singing along anyway. He throws his head
back and howls. The panes rattle in the sashes.

✦ ✦ ✦

"Here," Taconnelli says. "Here are your shoes back."

The rain begins to come down hard on Centralia now. The steam moves past the window, and there is a smell of sulfur. Taconnelli goes to the mountain of shoes, and lifts two into the air.

He hands me back a pair of long Aladdin's lamp slippers with long curling toes. There are little brass bells on the end.

✦   ✦   ✦

The blue color of my boot has disappeared into this grayish cocoa. Taconnelli smiles, watching the bells on the toes sway back and forth.

"See," he says. "I told you you wouldn't recognize them."

✦ Invisible Woman

My mother died of the laughing disease on the day that President Kennedy was assassinated, and for the next few weeks I suffered from the delusion that the American people were in mourning for her. In December I asked my aunt if we could go to see the eternal flame, but she just sighed and muttered something about my digestion. We proceeded in this manner until Christmas Eve day, when I was at last distracted from my grief by the arrival of the invisible woman.

Asking only that she be afforded some privacy, the stranger—wound from head to foot with horse bandages—came up the stairs melting snow on herself and dripping water on the rugs. My aunt led her to the second-most-distant room in the house. This had formerly belonged to my mother, and still clung vaguely to her fading smell. (My mother, through no fault of her own, had often exuded the fragrance of crayons.) The invisible woman, much to our relief, disappeared into my mother's room and was not heard from again until New Year's Eve, when she was observed knocking icicles off of the rain gutter with a window pole while singing the lyrics from some mournful German opera.

On the day that the invisible woman arrived, I had spent the morning watching a group of eight-year-old boys light garbage on fire. Before my mother died, the boys—we called ourselves the Visigoths—had used our basement as headquarters. I had become a Visigoth the previous August through a ceremony that included the drinking of diluted bleach and the intonation of what was supposed to be a chant in the language of Dalmatians. Since that time, I had been present on those occasions when the Visigoths went out in the world to light garbage on fire or to shoot badgers and turtles through the head with ball bearings, BBs, and walnuts.

My mom was buried in the Odd Fellows cemetery, on the slopes of the hill that led up to the dump where the garbage was burned. It was pretty up there, up on the hill with the lilacs and the honeysuckle, and the headstones tilting at strange angles. The brownstone tombs were crowned with winged skulls and hollow-eyed goblins. From where my mother was buried, you could see all of Centralia, Pennsylvania, even

72

beyond Centralia to Ashland and Mt. Carmel. You could see the steeple
of the Greek Orthodox church, and the silo of Moogus's farm. Moogus
bred mink, so it was never quite clear what the silo was for. Next to
Moogus's was the Wawa, where you could buy rock salt, scrapple, and
rubber cement.

The Visigoths had avoided my mother's grave when we went to burn
garbage, but I had been too distracted by the thought of the approaching
explosion to think of her. We poured barbecue fluid on the old sofas and
the newspapers and the twisted mining equipment and took turns
throwing matches. I have never felt so alive, so joyously and consumingly
absent-minded, as when the sofas glowed red, and the thick flames
rushed above the melting snow.

The fire, unfortunately, did not burn itself out from week to week, but
glowed patiently in anticipation of its next transfusion of barbecue fluid.
On the day before Christmas the fire reached an arm of the Ashland coal
vein which was close to the surface of the junkyard and began threading
its way through the mines and veins beneath Centralia.

Twenty-two years later Centralia was evacuated and demolished by
order of the Department of the Interior. The fire, working with the speed
of winter sap through an old tree, snaked under the graveyard, across
Locust Avenue, beneath the church, under the mink farm, under the
Wawa. The smoke that poured from the boreholes on Locust Avenue the
day they came to demolish our house—the last Sunday in January,
1984—was from the same fire that first met life two decades before, in the
matchboxes of the Visigoths.

The funeral had taken place on the day Jack Ruby shot Lee Oswald.
My aunt took my hand as we left the cemetery. Aunt Kate was a nervous
woman, always cracking her knuckles and blinking. That morning after
the funeral we went to the Greenway diner in Ashland, where my aunt
had scrambled eggs and scrapple. The scrapple made her sick. I used to
ask her what was in scrapple. "Everything but the squeal," she'd say.
When she got an Alka-Seltzer at the diner I remember thinking the
reason the water was fizzing was because my effervescent aunt was
drinking it.

Aunt Kate put an ad in the *Shamokin News-Item* two weeks after the
funeral: LARGE COUNTRY INN NOW LETTING ROOMS. Within a month the
old, cavernous house in which I had lived alone with my mother and my
aunt had become a hotel teeming with strangers. I felt as if a tornado had
passed through town—leaving such pictures as one saw in *Look* and

Boy's Life—with the cows stuck in the attic and shafts of corn impaled through telephone poles. My aunt nailed numbers on all the bedroom doors. My room became number seven.

It was soon with a great dread that I passed the closed door of number eight, the invisible woman's domain. The room was almost always silent, except when she could be heard singing her little song. She arranged with my aunt for her meals to be sent up to her and left outside her door. She requested to be served only beige food and thus survived for several months on a diet of chicken à la king, hash, and slightly chocolate milk.

Her baby was born on Flag Day. I had been unfurling the flag from the widow's walk when the house began to echo with the pains of her labor. My aunt had a quick talk with the midwife concerning whether it might not be educational for me to witness a birth (for my aunt was a liberal and had learned to use a walkie-talkie during the Spanish Civil War), but in the end wisdom prevailed and I was sent to the study, where for six hours I watched the launching of *Gemini 5* on television.

Seven months to the day after my mother had died we stood in the cemetery again, watching them bury the invisible woman's baby. The invisible woman stayed behind, at the hotel, while my aunt and Reverend Bickford and the Lutheran choir observed the interment. The Lutherans liked to make a big deal over things, but because so little happened in Centralia—prior to its demolition—they rarely got the chance. Smoke from the mine fire drifted from the junkyard and hung in the air above the cemetery.

It was a clear June day, and some of the flowers were almost out. While the tiny casket was being covered up I went over to look at my mother's grave. The Lutherans were singing "O God Our Fath'r." The smell of smoke stung my eyes.

Everyone expected the invisible woman to go back to wherever she had come from now that her baby had been born; my aunt was actively hoping for this, for her presence in the hotel was beginning to give the place a bad name. My aunt thought she had given the resident of number eight a good deal; no one had asked after her identity, in spite of the obviousness of her sin and the grotesqueness of her attempt to conceal herself. All that remained now, my aunt said, was that she make her exit with dignity and silence. The days passed, however, and still the invisible woman remained.

Other guests, perhaps attracted by the rumors my aunt had hoped to repress, began to arrive. There was a Mr. Irvine, who claimed to have caught the disease that killed the dinosaurs, and a Mr. Peeler, whose feet secreted a brownish juice. A Mr. Garfield, who wore white linen suits, suffered from erethism. He wouldn't explain what erethism was, but we could tell from the way he wound spaghetti round his fork that it made him nervous.

One of the guests—a Mr. Schneider—was already familiar to me. He was the husband of the woman who had been our elementary school teacher the previous year. She had run off with the youngest of the Niemeyer triplets (the one who ran the Ashland Snack Shop) in the autumn, so three weeks into school we had to forget that we had ever heard the name of Mrs. Schneider and memorize the name of Mrs. Bassoon, who had no neck. Mr. Schneider, who had worked for the coal company for thirty-five years, had expected to spend his declining years eating his wife's potato pancakes, but instead he found himself in a third-floor room, alone, making belts and ties out of aluminum flip-tops. I pitied Mr. Schneider but was also glad he was around, because he gave me things that he had woven, including a flip-top vest with three tiny pockets.

The invisible woman finally left the house in July, two days after I saw her without her disguise. On this same day I had accidentally driven my bicycle off of a cliff and wound up getting a huge bump on my head and got yelled at by Mrs. Sagg, the woman my aunt hired as a cook for the hotel, and was unable to remember anything except the names of horses for a week and a half. I would not have minded this except one of the guests in the hotel, a Mr. Sheckles, was a gambler, and kept hovering over me, convinced that I was, somehow, the key to his fortune.

The day was the Fourth of July, 1964. At eleven-thirty in the morning the Visigoths were traveling at thirty-five miles an hour down the hill on Locust Avenue. We were ringing the bells on our bicycles and yelling swearwords. Years later the highway we were speeding down would have to be closed because the mine fire crept directly underneath the hill and caused the road surface to bend and buckle, like a sausage left too long in the pan.

A diesel Mack, belching black smoke and blowing its nose, swung around a bend in the road which the adults called Suicide Corner. Most of the Visigoths had the good sense to get out of its way. This wisdom, however, was not shared by Jimmy Mashmire, who had a purple birthmark on his head. You could see it underneath his crewcut, and years later one would have thought of Mikhail Gorbachev. He wobbled directly in front of me, and I lost my balance. My bike bumped over the gravel, bounced once in a drainage ditch, and soared off the edge of Suicide Corner into space.

My bike and I separated several feet off the edge. Below me was a lake, some rocks, and the hurtling form of my Schwinn burning up as it re-entered the atmosphere. Behind me was the edge of the cliff, the interested faces of my fellow Visigoths, and the honking enormousness of the tractor-trailer.

I was not killed by my flight through space. Some people say the benefits of space travel aren't outweighed by the risks and the cost, but I am not one of those people. I landed in the midst of Suicide Lake, and after a brief check the Visigoths decided that I had traveled through some kind of pothole in the space-time continuum. We fixed the bicycle, and soon enough we were walking back up the hill toward Centralia, where downtown there was a parade and picnic and the Boulton Brothers Pennsylvania Carnival.

We merged into the parade between a float with a cow on it and the high school marching band from Mt. Carmel. The band was loud, being made up of about eight brass instruments and twenty-five drummers. We marched along to those drums while people on the sidewalks of Locust Avenue waved old flags at us. Most of the flags had been around since before the war and had only forty-eight stars.

The parade emptied into the camping grounds on the edge of town, where the Boulton Brothers Carnival was pitched. We snuck into the carnival by slipping under the flap of the tent where they kept the laughing hyena, a dying animal that didn't move unless one of the Boultons force-fed it coffee and jolted it with electricity.

We ate cotton candy that turned our tongues purple. We stood in line for Pennsylvania Dutch funnel cakes, and we got popcorn that came in boxes that we threw at people from the top of the Ferris wheel. I got stuck with Jimmy Mashmire on the wheel and swung the car to make him cry. There were stories about people who had died from doing this. We did not die, but there was a sign at the bottom of the wheel next to the generator that read: If You Stand Here While Wheel Is Turning You Will Be Killed.

I liked the view from the top of the Ferris wheel, horrifying as it was. You could see the steam escaping from the pit behind the cemetery; you could see the cranes at the top of the hill raising and lowering their shovels. At the time there was the hope that a process called fly ashing would stop the spread of the fire. That was what the cranes were doing: spreading fly ash. Beyond the "ashworks" (as we called it later) was the widow's walk of my house and the collapsing silhouette of Moogus's mink silo. There was the long decline toward Ashland, and the hills and mountains beyond that. Everything stretched toward the horizon, beyond which lay Scranton and Wilkes-Barre and Reading and Bethlehem and Erie.

Big kids from the high school were shooting photographs of the governor with popguns. Blindfolded coal miners used air guns to propel bean-bags through funnel cakes. Women in curlers threw darts at balloons. The principal of the high school guessed the number of beans in a jar.

I stood under an elm tree drinking lemonade and watched a helium balloon someone had lost get smaller and smaller.

We blew the last of our money getting in to see the freak show, where the Monkey Boy mushed some bananas through his teeth.

In the afternoon we returned to my house to steal some food. We found some leftover potato salad along with some raw scrapple, and we screwed the heads off of some statues that belonged to Mr. Sheckles, the gambler. The statues were whiskey flasks disguised as American eagles and John Kennedys and Elvises. We drank some of the whiskey out of Elvis and washed it down with orange Hi-C and played hide-and-go-seek. Jimmy Mashmire, the boy with the birthmark, was It.

Soon he was counting up to ten thousand by fives.

Steve Graves disappeared behind a stack of books. Richie Bernhart got inside the hamper in the second-floor bathroom. Al Ponkney and Buddy went up to the third floor to Mr. Sheckles's domain. And I went into my mother's room for the first time since the bandaged woman had come to Centralia. I hid behind a garment bag in my mother's closet. The garment bag smelled like mothballs and crayons and looked like an iron lung.

Jimmy's footsteps came down the hall. A door opened. I lurked in the closet behind the curtain of my mother's clothes, waiting for the sound of his steps going up to the third floor.

Something creaked in the bathroom; I pictured Richie Bernhart squirming in the hamper. The bathroom door opened. Richie was making his move.

The door to my mother's room opened, and I stood very still.

The footsteps came into the room and stopped, as if someone was listening for me. Light crept into the closet through the crack under the door. A long shadow passed by.

The footsteps went to the bed and back. I heard the sound of the door close. It locked.

Someone sighed. A tuneless voice hummed softly in a foreign tongue. The closet door opened.

She muttered softly to herself. A gauze bandage trailed on the floor beside her feet. Someone knocked on the door to the room and found it bolted. "Hey," Jimmy shouted, "No fair. Open up."

A hand reached to the floor and picked up the bandage.

"Come on," Jimmy said, "Who's in there?"

She turned. There was a pause as the invisible woman reaffixed the bandage to her face, then opened the door.

"What is it you desire?" she whispered.

I heard a polite scream, then the sound of feet on the stairs. The door to the room was closed again, but I did not hear the tumblers of the lock.

She sat down on the edge of my mother's bed. She had left the closet door open, and I could see her sitting there, very still, her hands folded in her lap. She slowly leaned back in bed, and rocked her feet. The monotonous voice again began to sing.

She reached to her face and began, once more, to remove the bandages. I could hear her muffled song. It was "My Grandfather's Clock."

She reached around the back of her head to undo a clasp that held the bandage. She had cold eyes and a face that seemed to have had all the color drained out of it.

In my mind I heard the voice of my former teacher, the woman whose memory had had to be supplanted by the neckless Mrs. Bassoon; I remembered the expression in her eyes as she walked into class, smiled cruelly, and said: "All right, get out a sheet of paper and number it from one to fifty."

Things had not worked out between Mrs. Schneider and the youngest of the Niemeyer triplets.

Mrs. Schneider got up and walked toward the window. While her back was turned, I moved as quickly and quietly as I could toward the door.

She stood looking out the window toward the Odd Fellows cemetery, humming softly to herself. I pulled on the doorknob. It turned around and around in my hand, but the door remained locked. Mrs. Schneider turned to look at me and gave a soft cry. Then she started to walk toward me.

GET OUT A SHEET OF PAPER AND NUMBER IT ONE THROUGH FIFTY. I fell to the floor and began to sob. I banged and banged on the floorboards but no one came; the Visigoths had other concerns.

She reached down and picked me up. She sat down on the bed and held my neck with her fingers. I waited to feel my neck snap like a finger in a lobster's claw, but I only felt Mrs. Schneider's fingers on the back of my neck. She was still singing "Grandfather's Clock," although now she was beginning to insert a few German words into the lyrics.

She pressed a key into my hands, and I looked up at her. She ran her fingers through my hair, then turned away.

I left the room with my head beginning to ache from the bump I had gotten when I fell into Suicide Lake. When I got to the first floor, I found that the other Visigoths had given up on me, leaving only a small note that said We Waited and Waited. My bicycle lay alone in the front yard, and I thought of the sign I had seen: If You Stand Here While Wheel Is Turning You Will Be Killed.

All of this happened over twenty years ago in a town that no longer exists. Just before the government came, there was a movement to have the entire town transplanted, house by house, to a new location. Centralia was to be a true Phoenix, reborn in the folds of two strip-mined mountains just south of Mt. Carmel. But somebody found out how much this would cost and somebody else decided he wanted to change his neighbors anyway, given the opportunity, and soon we were all dispersed across the face of Pennsylvania, some even farther away than that.

I climbed on my bicycle and went off to find my friends. Halfway to the mailbox, though, I looked back up at the house. The invisible woman was observing me, watching me recede with a look of lost, hopeless love.

I was filled with a lightness, a reckless weightlessness that made my innards throb. As I rode away from home I realized it was the same feeling I had had earlier in the day, when I had sailed without fear, without gravity, off the cliff at the edge of the world.

✦ The Love Starter

Doreen didn't even like her Uncle Flip. That was the ironic part. She had never found his eccentricities endearing, nor was she interested in his tedious, circular fabrications. He called himself Flip Carter, "The Love Starter." And yet it was Doreen he had come to, almost a year and a half ago, desperate, begging for her to be what he called his "contact." There was a wild look in his eyes, as if he were a calf that had been lassooed. She said she would help.

Since that time, as far as the rest of the world was concerned, Uncle Flip had vanished. No one knew whether he had been kidnapped, or swept out to sea by an unexpected undertow, or if he had jumped into the Great Crater Lake, or joined the merchant marines, or what. No one, that is, except for Doreen, who alone knew that her Uncle Flip, her late father's brother, was now on a mountaintop overlooking a fishing village on the northern coast of Nova Scotia, living in a doghouse.

The job was not difficult. He had given her twenty thousand dollars. She was supposed to pay the rent on his house in Baltimore, pick up his mail, read it, throw it away. Doreen wasn't sure what it was he was doing in the doghouse, didn't want to know. It was something he just had to work out.

So she paid his bills, which came to very little because he wasn't home, and read his mail, which was not interesting. No one suspected Doreen of being her uncle's contact, because she was widely considered boring due to her inability to maintain a relationship with a member of the opposite sex. So it had gone, uneventfully, until April, which was when the hand arrived.

The postman left the package by the door. You could tell there was something about it. Doreen made some coffee, poured it down the sink, got out the bourbon. Doreen loved to drink, but it wasn't a problem.

It was wrapped up in newspapers and came with the simple message "yours." The hand itself appeared to have been severed from the arm of a young woman. It was well manicured in spite of its being bodyless and wore a modest diamond ring. Doreen wanted to take the ring off and look for an inscription but didn't want to pry. The hand clasped a small stone, perfectly round, as if washed by the sea. The fingers were frozen around it.

The presence of the hand, rather than filling Doreen with any particular horror, instead inspired in her a kind of tired exasperation with her uncle. After all, she had agreed to pay his rent for as long as he decided he wanted to live in a doghouse in Nova Scotia. She had not agreed to become the recipient of dismembered body parts. How to interpret it? Was it a warning of some kind—the threat of a blackmailer unaware that Uncle Flip had flown the caboose? Or, as the message said, did the hand belong to him, and was now being returned by someone who had had it out on loan? The entire affair was boring, and with exhaustion Doreen threw the hand into the trash in Uncle Flip's kitchen.

But that was the problem. No one took out her uncle's trash, so, if she just left the hand there, she would have to return sooner or later and dispose of it herself. And then, once outside, some dog might find it and then there would be a tremendous to-do and everybody would get nervous.

Which was why Doreen had taken the hand back to her house and put it in a drawer under the spice rack. For a while this was good solution. Out of sight, out of mind. Yet it was never out of mind, not really. Her food began to taste strange to her, as if odd spices, or unnatural amounts of the regular ones, were working their way in. She thought that this was just her own nervousness until a man named Simon she had invited over after work also noticed it. He had gone into the kitchen after dinner to help wash up, and then there they were, Simon kissing the back of her neck, Doreen drying the cups and saucers, and the hand, clutching its little stone, lying in the drawer beneath the spices.

Simon hadn't found the hand but he might have. Eventually he stopped calling and the reason for that was probably that she didn't really feel very attractive. How could she, what with someone's hand less than two feet away all the time? How could you think? Anyway, the hand had to go. It would have to be destroyed.

But she couldn't destroy it. Let's say she burned it. That would leave the bones, and these would have to be discarded on the sly anyway, so why bother? The thing, then, was to leave it somewhere, some handlike place. But what if her fingerprints were on it? Can you get fingerprints on a hand? What if its fingerprints were on her? That's how they would trace it.

The solution was bothersome but obvious. She'd have to find Uncle

Flip and let him deal with it. She was out of her league. Anything else would implicate her. She would become an accessory after the fact, and Doreen, of all people, did not wish to be an accessory to anything. She took a week's leave of absence from the law firm, packed her belongings, and got in the car. She wished, as she set out on her trip, that she had someone to talk to about the things that were in her heart, someone like Simon only with more faith, but because there wasn't anyone she did not.

Three days later she was in Calais, Maine, across the river from Canada. She parked her car in the lot of a cheesy motel, next to a pickup truck that had New York plates and a bumper sticker that said I Like Milk.

The motel was perched on the arm of the Calais peninsula, where the St. Croix River met the Bay of Fundy. There was a lighthouse on the opposite shore, a small blue structure with a rotating orange light. Every twelve seconds the light made Doreen's room glow. She did not mind this, except that she became obsessed by the delusion that one time she would open her eyes to see the outline of some man standing in the shadow.

There was a soft sound, like the chirping of a cricket, from somewhere within the room. Doreen sat up in bed. The lighthouse flashed. The sound came again. It seemed to be coming from her suitcase but this was not possible. Not unless it was snapping its fingers. What was she supposed to do, wait upon it hand and foot?

She opened her suitcase, pulled back the newspaper. The hand had not dropped its rock. The lighthouse flashed again.

"Jesus Christ," Doreen said, and pulled on a pair of jeans and sneakers. She locked her room behind her and went outside.

The hotel pub was almost deserted. A few men wearing hunting caps were watching television with the sound off. A tired barmaid got Doreen a beer as a radio played some songs in French.

At the bar next to her was an extremely thin man with John Lennon glasses. He had an aquiline nose that soared out in front of him. He was not bad-looking, but something about him was not quite right. He wore a T-shirt that said I Like Milk.

"Oh, you're the one from New York," Doreen said, not expecting to speak out loud. He looked over at her. "Your car," she said. "I noticed the sticker."

"Yeah, well, it's my uncle's car," the young man said, waving his hands with sudden effusion. "His T-shirt, too, I don't really have anything to do with milk per se, my uncle, he used to be a dairy farmer, now he's just retired, see, anyway, both the shirt and the thing on the car, it's just a gag, you know. I mean milk's neither here nor there to me. I'm from Newtown Square. Pennsylvania. You're not from around here, are you, I can tell, the way you speak. That's not your car out there parked next to mine, is it? The one from Maryland?"

"Yes. Yes, it is."

"Where are you from in Maryland?"

"Baltimore."

"Is that nice?" he asked.

"Yes," she replied. "It's nice." She smiled. "Baltimore." She wondered if he was going to turn out to be insane. "You know they call it 'Charm City.' "

He was looking at his beer.

"You know, like how New York's the Big Apple, and Boston is Bean Town. Baltimore is Charm City."

He looked up at her. "I'm sorry, what were you saying?"

"It was nothing," she said.

He smiled. "I'm sorry, I'm nervous," he said. "I have to fly tomorrow, I'm a little wound up."

"You're afraid of flying?" she said.

"It's not just that. See, there's this whole long story that goes with it. I don't want to bore you."

"That's okay," Doreen said. "I don't bore."

To Doreen's regret the young man then cleared his throat and launched into a complex story. It was as if he'd been rehearsing it for hours. As he spoke he looked at his reflection in the mirror behind the bar. He did not look at Doreen.

"See, there's this threat of death on me," he said. "A curse. Not by anyone in particular, just somehow it got there." He cracked his knuckles. "It started last week. This old girlfriend of mine calls me up, she goes: 'Listen, Russell, I'm glad you answered the phone, but I should ask you, are you aware of what's going on?' I go: 'What do you mean, what's going on?' She goes: 'Listen, I don't want to scare you or anything, but there's this rumor going around among your friends that like you've been killed.' Can you believe that? Like out of nowhere she bumps me off."

"Yes," Doreen said. "I can believe that."

"Anyway, I hung up on her, didn't think too much about it, then that night I went to see a play, and while I was watching it I was thinking about the effect of what goes on in people's minds has on what happens in the world. Did you ever hear that thing about if every person in China jumped off of a one-foot-high stool at the same moment, the resulting impact would be enough to send the earth out of its orbit? That's what I'm trying to get at. Like what's the effect of all those former girlfriends of mine out there thinking that I've died somehow? Is that enough to make it happen? Probably not. First of all, there's probably only fifteen or twenty people at most who heard this. So what's that do? It's not enough to kill me. It's enough to what? Say, give me a headache. Or maybe make me sleep too late one day. I guess it would have more impact if they were all thinking this at the same time. Anyway, I'm thinking all this, watching this play, when suddenly this big ceiling tile, and I mean a big one, comes soaring out of the ceiling and hits me on the head. Hit the woman next to me, too; it was big. I had to go home, got a big lump on my head that was there the next day.

"Now I'm thinking: is this the way it starts, or is this the way it ends? I mean is that the end of the curse, or is this just the beginning?"

He paused to take a long drink from his beer, then looked over at Doreen with a big smile. There was something charming, yet also slightly unpleasant, something false, about him. Like he was nice enough in general, but used his articulateness as a means of covering up the fact that he collected worms or something.

"See, I'm afraid it's just the beginning," he said. "And tomorrow I've got to fly. I know something's going to happen. It's got to. So I was just sitting here, thinking about this thing. Somehow I've got to find a way to get uncursed. Before tomorrow."

The waitress came by and Doreen ordered another drink for herself. "And one more round of whatever this gentleman is having," she said. She snapped her fingers.

"Sorry, we're closing up," the barmaid said.

"Aw, come on," Doreen said, "Can't we get something first? I could use a shot of bourbon and another beer."

"Sorry miss, we're closed. Pay up now."

"You really drink that stuff?" Russell said.

"Uh-huh," said Doreen. "An old boyfriend of mine used to drink it."

"Well, you know, I've got a bottle of Old Grand Dad if you want. Back in my room. I mean, I don't want to say the wrong thing or anything."

Doreen smiled. Saying the wrong thing seemed like the last thing this Russell was worrying about.

So they were sitting on the edge of his bed drinking Old Grand Dad straight from the bottle. Russell had not finished his story. "Yow," Doreen said. "This stuff is good."

Russell shrugged and said, "Uh-huh." He was suddenly shy, strangely awkward. Doreen sized him up: All Talk.

"I think I should open a window," he said, and got up. He rolled the metal handle, opening the room up to the full force of the ocean breeze.

"Jesus Christ," Doreen said, as papers blew off the desk. "Close that up, will you? Please?"

Something swooped into the room. It was large and gray and had enormous black wings.

"Good God, what is that?" It was flapping around the ceiling.

"It's a vulture," Russell said. "It's the curse. This is it. Oh my God."

"It's not a vulture," Doreen said. "I think it's an owl."

"An owl! Jesus, that makes it worse!"

"Shoo!" Doreen said. The owl opened its talons and swooped around their heads.

"Let's get out of here!" Russell said. "Come on!"

Doreen grabbed the bottle of Old Grand Dad and followed him out the door.

"Well that's just great," Russell said. "Now I can't even sleep."

"It'll find its way out again," Doreen said. "Give it enough time."

She took a slug from the bourbon bottle. "Yow," she said, and handed it to Russell.

"In the meantime," she said, "why don't you come back to my room? In the morning the owl or whatever it is will be gone. And then we can be on our way."

She looked at him, then leaned forward and kissed him on the lips.

"Yow," he said.

At three in the morning, Russell was asleep, his head resting on her breast. Outside, the lighthouse was still pulsing. She thought that what she had feared before had come to pass, except that the man's shadow wasn't in the lighthouse flash anymore. Now it was on her.

Russell raised his head and kissed her. She touched his ear. "Doreen," he said. "Will you marry me?"

She smiled, but something in her feared that Russell was not kidding.

He was the kind of man who, once you slept with him, went completely berserk. Soon he would be sending her things, telling her stories, and giving her nicknames until she couldn't remember who she was anymore.

She would have to get up before him in the morning. It was difficult but easier than you'd think. Most of them just keep snoring if you give them the opportunity. It would be rude, of course, but she had no choice. Not unless she wanted to start some whole thing, and she couldn't do that. She'd just have to get out, get in the car and cross the border, cross the bridge over into another country. It was the simplest thing in the world, to just be up and on your way.

She fell asleep to the lighthouse flash, and listening to the sizzle of the round stones as they rolled against the shore. The ocean was covered by a deep fog. There was a gray cliff dotted with sheep and sheepdogs. Her uncle stepped out of the doghouse and shook his head. "I knew if I sent it to you, you would come," he said. "I knew you'd have to join me. I get so lonely up here, by myself, with no one to tell my stories to. I'm so glad you're here."

"But the hand—" she said. "Whose hand is it?"

The round stone fell from the palm onto the beach, where it was lost among thousands of others. "I thought I told you," he said. "It's yours."

✦ Aloe: *Part Three: The Making of "Aloe"*

for Dan McCabe

Aloe is a "performance novel" narrated by a man who, at irregular intervals, wakes up from a deep sleep laughing his head off. The thing that he finds so hilarious while he is dreaming immediately vanishes from his mind the moment he opens his eyes, and the narrator (Aloe) lies awake in the darkness of the pasteurizing room (for he lives in an abandoned creamery) with the humorous but puzzling residue of the dream world dying on his lips.

The laughter Aloe emits while dreaming is not his own. Aloe's laughter is high and lyrical; the laughter that comes out of his sleeping lips is robust, like that of a cigar smoker. Because Aloe can never remember what it is his unconscious finds so funny, he assumes the jokes are being dreamt by someone else, whose sense of humor is unexplainably being transferred into his unconscious, like accidentally picking up local walkie-talkie dialogue on one's hi-fi.

Aloe's life is somewhat miserable (living as he does in the abandoned creamery) and humorless, and therefore he looks forward to his nocturnal tête-a-têtes with longing. Much of the performance novel is concerned with Aloe's search for the "unconscious alphabet of humorfulness"—an unconscious language that seems to express a certain joy that eludes Aloe during his hours of standing up and breathing and blinking his cow-brown eyes. Aloe hopes that by learning to think not in words but in the formless language of his laughing other he will find a new way of being, that he will begin evolving into what he calls the "Jokemaster"—an exceedingly amusing person of the Coming Age.

Obviously it would have been tedious to write *Aloe* in the exhausted language of postcontemporary fiction. It was clear to me that Aloe's quest could only be described using the very language sought by the novel's protagonist. And yet, the novel—which I envisioned as a sort of "little epic"—presented a problem; how to write a dream joke that exists beneath language, that ordinary English might only mar? How to circumvent verbs and nouns? Can you do it by barking?

In order to do justice to Aloe's predicament I realized I would have to shrink both of us down to the level of the dream world, then run us

87

through the enlargo-chamber in order to explain it back to this, the wakeful one. "In the eye of God, there is no zero," as Fussmucker has said, and yet to make the almost-zero my infinity would surely take a whopping heap of gumption. It was I who was dreaming Aloe, from this side of the fictional mirror, and yet some other person, the cigar smoker, was making him laugh.

My first step in preparing for the writing of *Aloe*, then, was to rid myself of human language, as well as of a pair of plaid pants I had received for Christmas from my grandmother, the woman who, when her house burned down, took the insurance money and spent six weeks in Tokyo. "I sought the language of the funny things," as Fussmucker wrote in *The New Waggishness*, "to see, if I could discover the antidote to my own vapidity, so that, when my time came to die, it would not be suggested that I had never been jocular." Now to lose all words altogether would be to become trapped on the other side of the reflection; so I had to retain as much language as would be necessary to remain human (and also to make myself understood by my cousin Aglet, who is in a drug-rehabilitation program).

I wrote most of *Aloe* in the mornings, before I had found my glasses. Before sleep I would prepare myself by writing down as many joke openings as possible. In the mornings, I would be overwhelmed by punch lines. Slow pygmies. A big red rock-eater. A newspaper. A sunburned zebra. A nun falling down the stairs. One to phone the electrician and two to make the piña coladas. One to screw it in and one to kick the stool out from under him. Chicken of the sea. That was the boyfoot bear with teaks of Chan. Thumbalina, thumbalina, tiny little thing. To get to the other side. The punch lines I found, however, rarely matched the jokes I had begun with the night before. Nevertheless, in this manner, I forced myself to grind out the rough draft of the work that later became known as *Aloe: Part One: "Aloe" Itself*. First draft in hand, I was at last ready to begin rewriting the entire thing backward.

I saw *Aloe* as a kind of biographical opera to be performed in the language of legumes and tubers. In the first act, for instance, Aloe is walking around the creamery trying to think up a scheme for getting rich. The chicken house is not in terrible condition, and occasionally he thinks about putting a new roof on. He could rent out the chicken house and the old farmhouse together to somebody, or perhaps open a video store in the springhouse. When he was a child, Aloe would slide off the springhouse's roof. He and the other kids would get wooden shingle splinters in their backsides. They would slide off the edge of the roof and land in heaped-up autumn leaves. It was dangerous, and one time Aloe landed on somebody else, who went home crying.

The taste of the water from the springhouse fills Aloe with a vast mumpishness. He stands there in the late morning, in the cool dark, letting the soft rusty water roll over the bottom of his mouth where the tongue's connected. His stepfather was found in the springhouse, about a week and a half after he had vanished. He had never been told if his stepfather had been killed here, had killed himself, or if he had merely been found. As a child he remembered his chief concern was that his stepfather had been found with his head in the spring pool, and as a result his mother and he had spent the last week unwittingly drinking him.

At the funeral this had seemed, to Aloe, like the funniest thing in the world. Drinking him. Now that you think about it, the water had tasted a little funny. Sort of like Tang. Which they took to the moon. Aloe thinks of his stepfather all crystalized into a powder and for sale in the Safeway in a little canister with his big smiling head pasted on the front like Chef-Boy-R-Dee.

There he is, sitting in the front pew next to his weird cousin Lydia, less than two feet away from the casket, trying to suppress his laughter. The more he thinks about it, the worse it gets. Lydia hears him laughing, and she begins to laugh, too. The two of them are sitting there in the front pew, trying not to laugh, aware that if they do so much as look at each other, or even hear each other trying to hold in the laughter, it will get even worse. Lydia is holding her nose, trying to keep from exploding. They are sitting in the front pew shaking up and down. Everyone thinks they are crying.

In the part of the novel where I show Aloe trying not to laugh in front of the casket, I draw an impressive and complicated mathematical formula, similar to this one:

$$L + (\text{Shrunken Head}) = \frac{\text{Twaddle}}{(\text{Repression})^2} + (\text{Shrunken Head})$$

Factoring out the shrunken heads, this leaves: L (Laughter) = the Twaddle divided by the Repression squared.

On stage this formula is presented in operatic form by the Thin Mathematician, obviously a stand-in for the author's neighborly side. Immediately after his aria, the house goes dark and a spot falls center stage. Rosco fog blows in from fans hidden in the wings. The Fat Man (the Anti-Aloe) enters, smoking a thick Macanudo cigar.

He is wearing loose clothing and a too-tight tie. His face is red, eggplanty. He is bald, except for some white tufts above the ears. He wipes his head with a handkerchief.

The Fat Man sits on a too-small stool. He lets his arms hang down and sighs. He makes soft gurgling sounds, and behind him on a video screen we see Aloe sliding off of the springhouse roof. There is a close-up in which we can see that the boy Aloe lands on is the Fat Man as a child. He gets up and goes home crying. It is not that being landed on by Aloe hurt so much as that all the other children think it is funny.

As the Fat Man recalls all this, he begins to weep. The tears he cries invoke the tears he cried in his room, that day years ago, when Aloe landed on him. He lay on his stomach and cried and cried. The more he cried, the more things he thought of that troubled him. Crying is like that: once you get started, you find yourself going through the entire larder of regret, seeing what else there is to eat. At moments when he seems to be winding down, coming to terms with his dejection, he deliberately thinks of the saddest thing he can (which in this case is Aloe's laughter, for the Fat Man believed that Aloe was his friend), and this brings a whole new wave of tears upon him, and he is overjoyed. The Fat Man, forty years later, still thinks of this sad afternoon when he needs to force himself to weep. His life is not sad: he has become a highly respected writer and editor of cookbook-mysteries. Yet the Fat Man uses this forgotten afternoon's sadness to give himself a kind of psychic Heimlich maneuver.

Aloe ends with the Fat Man and Aloe sleeping in two beds on opposite sides of a funhouse mirror. Aloe wakes up, laughing, suddenly morose and unable to remember what was so amusing back in the land of nonlanguage. The Fat Man gets into bed at this same moment and cries himself to sleep, feeling a kind of wistful joy in the process. The thing that Aloe cannot remember but that causes him joy is that sorrowful thing which the Fat Man cannot forget. It is that sad recollection of his childhood solitude that helps him to reach, each evening, the kind of peace that the creamery-imprisoned Aloe finds impossible.

Aloe was first performed at the Studio Theatre in Washington, D.C., on June 14, 1987. In true postcontemporary style, no audience was permitted in order not to interfere with the purity of the performance. In order not to interfere with the purity of the audience, no actors were allowed either. The whole thing took place in a vacant theatre and cost less than $400,000 to produce. The stage was designed to look like an old-fashioned hardware store with a wooden Indian in the front and a wooden horse next to him and a wooden cowboy next to that shooting him with a wooden rifle. The bullets were also wooden and were carved from the limbs of abandoned funhouse puppets.

The critics, like Aloe himself, have been divided. Some have praised *Aloe* for its unusual setting (although some have questioned the significance of the creamery), whereas others have been completely unmoved. Ebert (the big one) said it made him "laugh until he stopped." Siskel, however, warned that it might "shock the reader with its raw intensity." The most common complaint, though, is that something about the whole thing just seems too wooden. For my part, I have abandoned the form of the postcontemporary performance novel altogether and have returned to my project of writing the first edible cookbook-mystery/algebra test. The only recipe in the cookbook will be instructions on how to bake the mystery itself, which, although edible, is also, unfortunately, poison. Read backward, the cookbook is Aloe's life story. Entitled *Part Three: The Making of "Aloe,"* it begins with Aloe's earliest memory—a day before he lost his stepfather, when he took a full-length mirror from a guest room, and leaned it, tenderly, against his bedroom wall, in order to see if he looked happy while he was asleep.

✦ The String

James Clelland came home from the shrimpworks to find a box kite collapsed in ruins on his porch. A string ran from one of the shards of broken balsa up over the decaying railing and into the woods behind the house. Clelland picked up the string and began to follow it into the woods, amused by the delusion that, should he trace the string to its terminus, he might find himself as a child on the other end. It wasn't out of the question. Not completely, anyway.

When he was little his father had taken the family to Gravesend Beach near Erie, where his parents fished for lamprey and he had flown a box kite for six days. You don't see box kites any more, Clelland thought, as his house disappeared from view behind him. Kids don't know how to make them. Now they surf from the back of diesel trucks and throw those flying saucers.

The kite Clelland had made in 1949 had taken a week and a half to build. He bought the balsa wood at the Hobb-EE-Town on Twentieth Street in Erie, then ran all the way home with the wood in his back pockets projecting like the feathers of a peacock. He was so excited when he got home he forgot what he had been doing and immediately sat down and snapped one of the dowels in half. He spent the remainder of the afternoon fixing the broken dowel with a kind of tubed cement that was clear and made luminous spheres dance before his eyes, similar to the kind flashbulbs used to make before Kennedy got himself shot like an idiot.

The membranes of the box kite had been devised by stretching copies of the *Evening Sentinel,* which Clelland's father used to bring home from the fishmonger's. The kite smelled like the papers which smelled like his father who smelled like bad salmon. There used to be hundreds of fish in Lake Erie before the lamprey took over. Now it's all lamprey. Snakes with sucker disks for heads.

The string led through piles of broad oak leaves which crunched like old newspapers beneath his feet. The string wound twice around a hollow tree. If I ever have a son, Clelland thought, I'm going to tell him elves live in there. They fix your shoes.

Clelland's father had a Packard. Such an honest man, Clelland thought. He worked his whole life at the fish market and finally bought a Packard at age forty. The Packard was too big for the family; his mother was embarrassed by it. It exploded threateningly when it started and emitted a cloud of wet gas when it stopped. Whenever the Packard died on him, Clelland's father used to say, "Son of a bitch!" It was his favorite expression. He would hit his thumb with a hammer and he would yell, "Son of a bitch!" He would misplace his spectacles and walk around the house fuming, "Now where did I put those goddamn sons of bitches?" People don't swear like they used to, Clelland thought. Nothing's anything any more.

The string led over the collapsed roof of a deserted house. Trees grew through what had once been the living room. On the ground around the ruin were some old shutters, some broken plates and dishes, parts of the roof. This is where the witch lives, he would tell his son.

The string came down the other side of the house and led into a marsh. Clelland felt the mud around his ankles as he squashed into the glen.

The abandoned house reminds me of the house where the McGonikle sisters used to live, Clelland thought, hearing the seductive suck of the swamp around his shoes. The oldest was Carolyn, but people called her Toozy. The middle one was Emily, but she was known as Woogie. And the youngest was called Arnold. When he first met a man named Arnold, he had thought it was a woman's name.

Woogie was the cute one. He used to drive her around in his father's Packard. He had kissed Woogie on Route 18 overlooking Lake Erie, and she was so surprised she had punched a hole with her fist through the convertible top. As a result of this, Clelland's father took away his driving privileges. Two years later, Woogie married Hobson Wentworth, whose father owned the Flexible Rolling Mills. Clelland sent them dishes.

When they finally got to Gravesend, Clelland found that a large hole had been punched through the membranes of the box kite by the apex of his mother's beach umbrella. Clelland's father took the boy out to a cigar store, where they bought a newspaper for the child and a copy of *American Mercury* for his father. The next day, Clelland stayed in the hotel room fixing the hole in the kite while his mother and father sat by the ocean and turned from potato-beige to clown-red.

The string led out of the marsh and into a long line of pine trees. There was little light. Dead needles muffled his footsteps. He had the sense of being watched and turned to look behind him. The string led back into the bog.

The next day it had rained. The kite was finally finished and ready to fly; a harness of string encircled its throat like a pleasant noose. Then: the rain. Clelland's mother and father sat in the hotel room, not speaking, as he read comic books and looked heartbrokenly toward the window. At one point he had caught his father's eye, and his father had said, "The sun will come out tomorrow, Jim."

But the following day it had rained again. Clelland's father took them driving. They went to see a movie. Something with Veronica Lake. His mother had liked it. Clelland and his father had not. "Why doesn't she get a haircut?" his father had said.

The string led forward into a clearing, where teen-agers now apparently gathered to use their powers for evil instead of good. There were broken bottles and crushed beer cans and names carved into trees and a lot of old junk. There was the hull of a ruined automobile. The string led in the driver's window and out the passenger's side, where there was no door.

On the next to last day of vacation the sun had come out. Clelland stood on the beach with his father and his dog, Moogus. His father had held the kite for him.

"All right, Jim, run!" he had yelled when the wind came up.

Clelland ran in front of the ocean as the box kite left his father's hands and dragged and bounced along the beach. Clelland ran so long Moogus got tired. The dog sat down and looked at him as if he were an idiot.

Clelland's father ran up behind him and helped him wind the string back up.

"You have to run faster," he said.

They examined the kite. It was not ruined. They walked back again and once more Clelland's father held the kite. The wind came up. Clelland's father yelled. Clelland ran. The string began to tug on Clelland's fingers.

Great winds blew up. Clelland let out the string as the kite grew small. People stopped to stare. The string burned through Clelland's palm as the reel gyrated on the sand. Moogus barked.

Clelland's father went to the umbrella and came back smiling. "I got you these," he said. There were five more reels of string.

They tied them on, one after the other, and the kite rose up over Lake Erie, growing smaller until you couldn't quite find it right away if you looked at something else. Only a small white dot remained, pulsing against the blue sky, like a candle in the middle of the ocean.

Clelland walked forward through the woods and saw the light breaking through the pines. Of course, he thought, I'm at the great lake. I'm here at last.

He ran through the remaining trees and saw the vacuum of the waterfront. In the distance he saw two figures and a dog, their hands shielding their eyes from the sun, gazing toward heaven.

In the end the kite had simply vanished. Even he couldn't see it any longer, and it was time to go home. Clelland held on to a string that led into space. His father shrugged and said, "Let it go, son."

He let go of the string and watched it rise into the air, as if being reeled in from the other end by God. The string was withdrawn into the sky like a retracted shaft of sunlight, and then he and his father and Moogus were alone by the sea.

There are stories, Clelland thought, in which people travel through time. Stories in which radio programs from the past suddenly, inexplicably echo out of people's hi-fi's. There's a scientific explanation for it. The waves bounce off the moon, or something. This is the same thing. The kite has been circling the earth for forty years now. If the kite has come down, it's only logical that I must be somewhere else now, looking up at it.

Then it dawned upon Clelland: I am not going to find myself as a child at the end of this string. I am going to find myself as my own father. I am the son I never had.

Clelland's heart grew larger as he ran down the beach toward the figures. He had never felt the desire to run so deep within him; he felt as if he were running in a new way, almost with the diagonals of a gallop. Something in him wanted to get a bone. Get a bone and dig. His ears felt floppy.

He felt the warm sand between his paws, and ran up to the boy and his father. The two of them, standing like statues against the sea, did not look at him. Their gazes beamed like radar waves toward the string vanishing in the sky. Clelland felt rather touched.

"Ruff," he said.

✦ Jimmy Durante Lost in Antarctica

"I'm passing the joints on Fourteenth Street between Third and Fourth avenues. I peeps under the swingin' doors and keeps thinking that the swellest job in the world is the guy dat bangs away on da piano. I wants to be him."

✦ ✦ ✦

Sophia hadn't seen her Uncle Werner since the fiasco at her grandfather's funeral. People weeping and sobbing. Some leaning over the sealed casket, yelling at each other, throwing fistfuls of flowers torn from wreaths. The funeral director was standing on top of a chair waving his arms and shouting, as if he were trying to direct an incoming plane. Sophia's father grabbed her by the hand and said, "Come on, we don't have to listen to this." Uncle Werner yelling after them, "Go on and run. That's what you're like. Nothing ever makes a dent on you."

✦ ✦ ✦

The biplane bounces once on the ice and is airborne. He's trying to go around the world clockwise. Admiral Byrd already circled the poles by plane, but he went the other direction. "The world is like a clock. And a clock dat's a thing what goes clock-a-wise. For this Byrd to go around anti-clock-a-wise—it's humiliatin'!"

✦ ✦ ✦

A year after her husband left her, Sophia fell in love with a man named Timmons. The relationship was passionate, yet Sophia couldn't bring herself to sleep with him. The moment he unbuttoned her shirt, gazing into her eyes with warm desire, Sophia was filled with a paralyzing sadness, a freezing melancholy that made her turn from her new love and stare at some extreme corner.

✦ ✦ ✦

Captain Scott's *Journal*, Tuesday, January 16, 1912: Camp 68, Height 9760. The worst has happened, or nearly the worst. We marched well in the morning and covered seven and a half miles. Noon sight showed us in Lat. 89 degrees, 42 minutes South, and we started off in high spirits in the afternoon . . . About the second hour of the march Bowers' sharp eyes detected what he thought was a cairn; he was uneasy about it . . . half an hour later he detected a black speck ahead. Soon we knew that this could not be a natural snow feature. We marched on, found that it was a black flag tied to a sledge bearer; near by the remains of a camp; sledge tracks and ski tracks going and coming and the clear trace of dogs' paws—many dogs. This told us the whole story. The Norwegians have forestalled us and are first at the Pole.

✦   ✦   ✦

Timmons was understanding but impatient. "If you called me by his name," he said. "Would that make it easier? You go ahead. You call me Mark if you like. Whatever makes it easy." Timmons, in spite of his Harvard education, is a huge Batman fan. He has a bad habit of saying, "To the batpoles," or of calling himself "Boy Wonder." This sounds all the more complex when spoken in Timmons's ridiculous New England accent. "You don't understand," Sophia said. "I hate him. I don't want to think about him." Timmons kissed her cheek. "You already are," he said.

✦   ✦   ✦

A young singer named Jeanne Olson came into the Club Durant by mistake. She had been booked into a nightclub around the corner. Durante knew she was confused but had her sing for him anyway. A year later they were married, becoming "the happiest couple in show business."

✦   ✦   ✦

Sophia had six uncles and one aunt. The family name was von Flugelhopf. The three oldest uncles had married rich American debutantes after the war—daughters of a lawyer, a banker, and a real estate tycoon. The younger three uncles married a waitress, a secretary, and a riveter. Sophia's Aunt Ilse, the youngest, spent the war in Austria. She had fallen in love with a German flyer named Kampfen, who once made puppets in Köln. When Kampfen's plane was downed by American gunfire, Ilse sank into a morbid dementia. By the end of the war she was hospitalized in Berlin, diagnosed as schizophrenic.

✦   ✦   ✦

Durante's plane is believed to have crashed in the Queen Maud Mountains, the soft range that marks the end of the Polar Plateau and the beginning of the Ross Ice Shelf. If he survived the crash and stays near the wreck, we might be able to reach him within the week. If he went off into the waste, there's no telling what could happen. He may have to be given up for lost. "Dat's da conditions dat prevail!"

✦   ✦   ✦

Captain Scott's *Journal*, Wednesday, January 17, 1912: Camp 69. Temperature minus 22 at start. The Pole! Yes, but under very different circumstances from those expected. We have had a horrible day . . . there is that curious damp, cold feeling in the air which chills one to the bone in no time. We have been descending again, I think, but there looks to be a rise ahead; otherwise there is very little different from the awful monotony of past days. Great God! this is an awful place and terrible enough for us to have labored to it without the reward of priority. Well, it is something to have got here, and the wind may be our friend tomorrow.

✦   ✦   ✦

Twenty years after her grandfather's funeral, the phone rings in Sophia's apartment. Uncle Werner, his voice heavy with drink, wants Sophia to come visit him. Aunt Ilse is dead, of a seizure of the heart, on board a freight train headed for the East Coast. She has been cremated in Salt Lake City, and her ashes are being sent by Greyhound bus to Uncle Werner's house in Atlantic City.

✦   ✦   ✦

From *Current Biography*, 1946: Durante's "comeback," in 1943, after Hollywood had decided he was "through," was hailed by the reviewers who considered him one of the great clowns of the era. He "rode the crest" with the night-club, radio, and motion picture successes, beginning in March 1943, just a few weeks after the death of his wife [Jeanne], to whom he had been "singularly devoted." Durante had found relief for his sorrow in a return, for the first time in twelve years, to "intimate, free-style" night-club entertaining; he was a sensational success.

✦ ✦ ✦

We have reached the Queen Maud Range: the blue-white mountains that dissolve in the frozen sea. To our left is Mount Hope: gray against the crystal sky. Penguins walk upon the glacier at the mountains' feet. There is no sign of Jimmy Durante here.

✦ ✦ ✦

Sophia knew why Uncle Werner had called her, of all people. She was the one member of the next generation who most resembled her late aunt, on account of her own tendency toward melancholy. "So you get sad sometimes," Timmons had said. "Big deal. We all get sad. Don't let your uncle try to convince you you're a manic depressive. That's not the kind of thing you ought to get talked into. Believe me." At seven in the morning the sun shone through a twelfth-floor window onto Sophia's bed, and she lay awake, resting her head on Timmons's shoulder. All the von Flugelhopfs had some sort of problem. There was something in the blood. Sophia's grandmother had deserted the family shortly after they emigrated from Austria. She disappeared, was presumed dead, swallowed by an anonymous death somewhere in America. In 1972, Sophia's mother got a phone call from a woman named Keebler in Fort Worth. "I wanted to let you know your mother died. She's been living with my father since 1960. We didn't even know she had any family." Mrs. Keebler's father was an airline pilot with American. Sophia and her mother flew to Texas, stared at the body on the slab in the Fort Worth morgue. A Latin engraving in the lobby read: "Now is the Time When Laughter Draws to an End, for Here is the Place where Death Brings New Life to the Living." Timmons, the sun shining on his hair, whispers softly in sleep. "Oh please," he says. "Oh please, please, please."

✦ ✦ ✦

From *Antarctica, Land of Frozen Time*, by Roger A. Caras: Since longitude is a measure of time, and not just distance, the day's twenty-four hours all converge here as well. There is really no "time" at the Pole. No matter what your watch says, even if it has stopped, it is correct! Because the International Date Line terminates here, you can move from Saturday to Sunday by taking one step. Actually, there is only one day and one night per year. . . . If you were to take twenty-four steps to go around the Pole, you should change your watch one hour each step, backward or forward, depending on the direction you chose to walk. And of course, there is only one direction at the bottom—North. This is one of the two places on Earth from whence it is impossible to go toward either the East or the West.

✦ ✦ ✦

Captain Scott's *Journal*, Saturday, March 17, 1912: Should this be found, I want these facts recorded. Oates' last thoughts were of his Mother, but immediately before he took pride in thinking that his regiment would be pleased with the bold way in which he met his death. We can testify to his bravery. He has borne intense suffering for weeks without complaint and to the very last was able and willing to discuss outside subjects. He did not—would not—give up hope to the very end. He was a brave soul. This was the end. He slept through the night before last, hoping not to wake; but he woke in the morning—yesterday. It was blowing a blizzard. He said, "I am just going outside and may be some time." He went out into the blizzard and we have not seen him since.

✦ ✦ ✦

Sophia's Aunt Ilse, discharged from the hospital, came back to America and began to wander the country, searching for something. She would take a job waitressing for a few months, live with some man, then just as suddenly vanish again. In her vague travels she resembled her mother, the woman who would eventually turn up in the Fort Worth morgue. Ilse, once an artist, became a map maker. She traveled the country with a great steamer trunk, filled with her maps and drawings. You could always tell when Aunt Ilse was going to arrive because she'd send the trunk containing her maps on first. The last time Sophia saw her was right before her grandfather's funeral. It was confusing. She was with her then-boyfriend, a fireman who had a big felt hat and a large nose. "Well, I've given up on maps," she said. "Chucked'em. There's a scene in *Through the Looking-Glass* about a race of map makers that gets to be so good that they make the scale of the maps 1:1. The same size as the thing they are a map of. Except that the maps are blocking out the sun and killing the grass underneath. So they throw all the maps away and let the world serve as its own map." Aunt Ilse had a small harmonica she could play the blues on. "It's like that."

✦ ✦ ✦

Two men argue at a dinner party. "It's environment!" "It's heredity!" "I say, old boy, environment!" "Dash it all, heredity, I say!" "Environment!" "Heredity!" "One hundred quid says it's environment!" "Two hundred says it's heredity." "Two fifty and done." "Done." They shake.

Sophia's father, a product of sixty years of genteel living, looks one way. His brother Werner, a hard drinker, looks another, as Sophia realizes, stepping out into the street in Atlantic City. She hears the deep rasping voice. "It's my girly-girl," he says. She hasn't seen him since childhood, since the funeral. Now, standing at the top of the back stairs above the B&C Saloon on Atlantic Avenue, he seems very old. Hardbitten. He opens his arms wide and says, "Come here, you little lump of mud." Sophia, her heart going out to him, runs up the stairs two steps at a time.

✦ ✦ ✦

Captain Scott's *Journal*, Wednesday, March 21, 1912: Got within 11 miles of depot Monday night; had to lay up all yesterday in severe blizzard. Today forlorn hope, Wilson and Bowers going to depot for fuel.

✦ ✦ ✦

Uncle Werner and Sophia drink sixteen-ounce beers in front of an artificial fireplace. "That feels good, huh?" he says. "You know, your Aunt Ilse always loved you. She really did. She told me so." His face darkens. "You know we said we'd never forgive them, your father and all them other bastards. Running out of the funeral like that. Not as long as we lived."

"Uncle Werner," Sophia says. "I don't know what happened at grandfather's funeral. I remember a fight about the casket being closed or something. But it's over. Done. This isn't anything I can do anything about."

Uncle Werner's face brightens suddenly. "That's right." He puts out his hand to shake. "Good for you. Okay. Okay." They shake. "Sometimes I talk too much." He looks around.

"Aunt Ilse—" Sophia says.

"Oh, ja. She loved you. She did. She was so proud of you, teaching in the high school. She knew all about you. She wanted you to have her drawings. When she died. She knew you'd understand. Her paintings. I looked at them once, I couldn't make heads or tails outta them. But you.

You were her little niece. She knew you'd be able to see them the right way."

He looks up suddenly.

"I've got her in the closet. Your aunt. Would you like to see?"

"In the closet?" Sophia says.

"Yeah. Them ashes. I went up the bus depot and got her yesterday. I was thinking, all the traveling Ilse did by bus, now when she comes home the last time, she's still on the bus. The world is nuts, am I right?"

He moves toward the closet.

"Uncle Werner, I don't think I want to see the ashes."

"What? You don't love her? You don't want to see?"

"I love her. I just don't want to look. I'm afraid."

"I'm afraid too," he says, looking at the closet. "With her in there. I have her on the floor. In the package she came in. I'm afraid. What if she's mad?"

"You should have her buried. You know, get her out of the house."

"I will," he says. "My friend Ned at the Veterans Administration's payin' for it, too. But for now she's gotta stay. They can't bury her yet." He sits down, takes a swig of his beer. "Ground's frozen."

✦   ✦   ✦

DA RIME OF DA ANCHINK MARINER

It was an Anchink Mariner!
And it stops a-one of t'ree!
By your long long gray beard, and glitt-rink eye
Say howcome stops yuz me?

Gee, Weddin' Guest—it goes like this:
It's growin' wondrus cold!
Ice, mast-high, it's floatin' near
As green as emma-rold!

I killed an Al-ba-tross, I says,
Chez South Pole, dat's a fact!
Twas then I knew how ev-ry-one
Wants-ta get inta da act.

He went like one that has been stunned
He left this simple warnin'
—"Surrounded by assassins!"—, still:
He woke the morrow mornin'.

✦ ✦ ✦

"By the way," Uncle Werner says. "What ever happened to that guy? The one you married. You know. What's his face."

"Mark," Sophia says. "He's gone."

"He left you or you left him?" Uncle Werner says. "It makes a difference."

"He left me."

"Well, that was a mistake. You shoulda left him first. From what I heard he was no big treat. That's what your Uncle Slim said. Cold as ice. Are you listening to me? Never let them leave you first if you're only going to leave them later. That's my advice. Then they're the ones who have to work it out. See this way, you get stuck with all the junk. You leave first, he gets the junk. The guilt I mean. It's common sense." Sophia looks at the floor and sighs. Uncle Werner puts his beer down. "Ah, girly-girl. I'm sorry. You love him, huh? That's sad. Even if he was an asshole. My heart goes out to you. But you'll find somebody. I know. A sweet thing like you."

"It's not that I worry about," Sophia says. "It's the forgetting."

"Oh, the forgetting is the easy part. It's the living. That's the part you can't learn over. Take it from me. Not a day doesn't go by when I don't think about your aunt. I wish you'd known her. You would have liked her. It's the worst thing, Sophia. Nobody gets to live all their lives."

✦ ✦ ✦

Captain Scott's *Journal*, Thursday, March 22 and 23, 1912: Blizzard bad as ever—Wilson and Bowers unable to start—tomorrow last chance—no fuel and only one or two of food left—must be near the end. Have decided it shall be natural—we shall march for the depot with or without our effects and die in our tracks.

✦ ✦ ✦

The plane is found, crashed nose-first beyond the mountains on the polar plateau. It seems to have exploded upon impact. There is debris everywhere: shards of the fractured propeller, large felt hats, tubs for kerosene, a large red handkerchief, a single mitten. A pair of footsteps leads from a spot twenty feet south of the wreck and into the snow.

✦ ✦ ✦

"Wait a minute. You hear this song?" Uncle Werner puts a cassette in a tape deck and begins to play a Marty Robbins tune. " 'A white . . . sport coat . . . and a pink . . . carnation . . . . ' That was her favorite song. Last time she was here, she listened to that over and over again. I heard it again the morning she died. On the radio. That was when I knew. It was like that ESP. What does it mean? Some man she loved, and lost? That German flyer? Maybe something she wanted and could never have. That's the way she was. All that desire like some soda in a bottle that's all shook up. See, your aunt didn't understand how to be happy. People have to let go of things. Not her. She listened to that over and over again. Like she was trying to rub things in on herself. You take a lesson. Don't live that way. That's the way you make yourself a nutcake."

✦　✦　✦

I'm passin' the joints on the Ross Ice Shelf. I'm thinking the guy what flies around in an airplane with his girl has got ta have the swellest job what is. I wants ta be in love. I wants ta be him.

✦　✦　✦

Sophia gets home late at night, and there is Timmons, waiting. "I was thinking about what you said," she says. "We don't have to talk about this," Timmons says. "I mean now. We don't have to talk about this now." "It's all right," Sophia says. "I've been thinking about things. I'll be all right. As long as you keep waiting me out. I just have to let things fade." They embrace. "Everything takes longer than I think it does." "That's all right," Timmons says. "That's what I've been trying to tell you. I can wait. Nobody's going anywhere." He kisses her, then laughs like the Penguin: "Waak. Waaak. Waaaak."

✦　✦　✦

Captain Scott's *Journal,* Thursday, March 29, 1912: Since the twenty-first we have had a continuous gale from WSW and SW. We had fuel to make two cups of tea apiece and bare food for two days on the 20th. Every day we have been ready to start for our depot 11 miles away but outside the door of the tent it remains a scene of whirling drift. I do not think we can hope for any better things now. We shall stick it out to the end, but we are getting weaker, of course, and the end cannot be far.

It seems a pity, but I do not think I can write more.

✦　✦　✦

Durante's journal is found twenty feet from the wrecked plane. The pages are alternately burned from the explosion and frozen in Antarctic ice. At the end of the flight log is a blank page, then the final entry.

"Good night, Mrs. Calabash," it says, "wherever you are." His footprints, filling with snow, trail away and vanish toward the South.

✦ Final Exam

PLEASE DO NOT BEGIN THIS STORY UNTIL SOMEBODY SAYS TO.

QUESTIONS 50–55 REFER TO THE FOLLOWING PASSAGE:

Two young men found themselves conjoined by the presence of a medical school cadaver. Having nothing more in common than the cadaver and a mutual girlfriend, they gave the cadaver the woman's name and evacuated her thorax. They did not see the face until the ninth week of Anatomy, at which time the corpse seemed less like a human being than an invisible bond that held Messrs. Beck and Verdi in thrall.

The corpse was the author of a number of unusual properties. While dissecting the stomach, Beck and Verdi discovered a series of unpleasant articles, including a pair of earplugs, an ashtray bearing 10
the symbol of a budding orchid, a matchbook bearing the initials I.S.F., the sheet music for *La Traviata*, a faded train ticket, the shell of a small turtle, an olive soaked with what was determined to be three parts gin, one part vermouth, and the masticated remains of schoolroom blackboard chalk.

For their final exam, Beck and Verdi were asked to determine the cause of death. Beck's verdict was indigestion. His thesis: victim had unusual combination of physical condition and neurotic impulses— namely, a compulsion for swallowing objects when pressured, and an extremely tough stomach. Beck imagined the following scenario: 20
victim—nicknamed Melanie Brown after Beck and Verdi's girlfriend—took a train to New York in order to have an affair. (The words "New York" were barely visible upon the ticket; it was not clear, however, if this were the destination or the point of origin.) Melanie Brown met a man in the city (the matchbook bore the faded message "8 P.M.—love, Inky"). She had presumably seen *La Traviata* and had had to take the subway back to the hotel. (The earplugs were the variety easily available from newsstands underground; the ashtray bore the orchid insignia of the Carlyle

106

Hotel on Seventy-sixth Street.) Melanie Brown had been poisoned 30
by a doctored martini by her lover, a man named Inky, and whose
initials, presumably, were I.S.F. An extensive but simple investiga-
tion of the Manhattan telephone book would reveal the name of the
murderer.

Verdi laughed long and loud at his friend's imagination. His
verdict: suicide. Melanie Brown was clearly married to a tyrant, a
man who not only loved opera (hence her consumption of La
Traviata) but who forced it off on his wife as well (hence the
earplugs). She had accompanied her ruthless husband to the
International Shoe Fair and stayed at the Carlyle, where she met 40
a man with whom she hoped to have an affair. She wrote down a time
to rendezvous on one of her husband's matchbooks; Melanie Brown
herself was Inky. Beck—somewhat bitterly—recalled from his
college days that Melanie had a large blue birthmark on her breast,
bearing some poetic resemblance to spilled ink; Verdi replied coldly
that he had never seen Melanie Brown undressed until the night of
his senior prom, when he had, unfortunately, seen everything in
duplicate; he was never able to envision Melanie Brown without
dividing her in half. Verdi's nostalgia notwithstanding, the devious
Melanie had clearly intended to poison her husband and escape on 50
the next train leading out of the city. Lacking the courage to
perpetrate the crime, Inky had killed herself by drinking the
poisoned martini she had prepared for her husband.

"Nincompoops," said the professor. "What about the turtle?
What about the chalk?"

"She was a school teacher with a very young child," said Beck.

"She was an animal trainer who played a lot of tick-tack-toe," said
Verdi.

"She was a neurotic," said the professor. "Who ate a lot of junk.
The liver shows signs of excessive drink. The fingernails bear the 60
trace of chromium oxide—the ingredient contained in the aerosol
germicide most commonly used to disinfect bowling shoes. The
subject drank too much and hung out in bowling alleys. No wonder
she died. Cause of death is stupidity. By the way, you both fail."

Several years later, Verdi—who took a job with the Egyptian
Embassy in New York—learned that Melanie Brown had died at
about the same time Beck and he had been dissecting the cadaver.
Melanie had become a collector of paste and lived in Greenwich,

Connecticut, working for the world's second-largest manufacturer
of mucilage. One day at work she had complained of strange pains   70
in her abdomen; her doctors found this causeless. She had died on
Arbor Day, attempting to express, on her deathbed, an incompre-
hensible remorse at the loss of some great and unforgettable love.

50. This is a story about:
    A) Two young doctors and the significance of indigestion
    B) The collusion of memory and interpretation
    C) The predestination of loneliness
    D) The subjugation of women

51. The "great and unforgettable love" in line 73 refers to Melanie
    Brown's love for:
    A) Beck
    B) Verdi
    C) Moe
    D) Nudd

52. The character Melanie Brown is most similar to is:
    A) Gerald McBoing-Boing
    B) Mr. "The" Toad
    C) June Lockhart
    D) Thomas Chatterton

53. The word "fail" in line 64 is a synonym for:
    A) Laying an egg
    B) Ending in smoke
    C) Working for the Egyptian Embassy
    D) Meeting one's Waterloo

54. This story could be called "pretentious argle-bargle" by a member of
    which of the following schools of criticism:
    A) Structuralists
    B) Culinary Institute of America
    C) Wharton
    D) "Read 'em and Weep" School.

55. If you were the author of this story, which of the following ought you
    try to do for a living:
    A) Breed Dalmatians
    B) Teach creative writing to clairvoyants

C) Go to one graduate writing program after another

D) Think up names for horses

QUESTIONS 56–60 REFER TO THE FOLLOWING PASSAGE:

Twenty years later Beck was watching the man at the controls of the backhoe filling up the Big Hole. Beck had moved into the house with the understanding that the Big Hole was a problem, but Beck's wife, Julie, had worried about it more than he did; she said it seemed to whistle to itself. It was not until Beck's son disappeared that he finally got around to calling the landscapers, who penciled him in for mid-June. Beck's son reappeared by May, but by then the days of the Big Hole were numbered. Now, everyone was standing around, watching the Big Hole disappear.

Several hours later Iggy got off the backhoe and attempted to   10
determine the Big Hole's depth with a plumb line. A low hollow sound, like someone blowing across the lip of a soda bottle, echoed from the Big Hole's depths.

"It sounds like the Devil," said Mrs. Weston.

"It sounds like someone snoring," said Mrs. DeWees.

"It sounds like a teakettle," said Mrs. Ogletree.

"I know what that is," said Iggy. "Do you know what that is?"

"What is that?" everyone said.

"This here hole goes straight through to the center of the earth and out the other side. That whistlin' is the sound of the air rushing   20
through here and comin' out in China."

"Australia."

"Australia?"

"Australia," said Beck's wife. "The other side of the world from here would be Australia."

"Whatever. It's deep."

"Nonsense," said Beck. "You're just trying to scare everyone to drive down property values. You get back on that Caterpillar and fill in that damn hole before you get pushed down it."

"No, sir," said Iggy."   30

"What do you mean, 'No, sir'?"

"I mean just what I say. That hole is a thing of the Devil, and I won't mess with it. You can take it out of my salary. I don't care. That thing is evil."

"You are an extremely silly man, and I will prove to you that the hole has a bottom by finding it myself." Beck retrieved a flashlight from his cellar, tied a length of nylon cord around his waist, and proceeded to lower himself into the hole. "I'll be back," he said, and disappeared.

Beck passed the roots of trees, some large rocks, and the houses of   40 what were probably elves. Still, the hole disappeared in continuing blackness beneath his feet. "I wonder if you can spray for elves," Beck wondered, remembering what the termites had done to the foundation the previous spring. Upon closer inspection, Beck found that the houses were made of sheet metal and were painted industrial green and blue. "Dollhouses," Beck thought. "It's some kids' dollhouses. Of course there are no elves. Don't be a jerk."

With a sudden jerk the nylon cord came to an end. Beck looked up; the light of the earth was just a spot now, like a hole in the roof of an opera house. Beck felt himself rising for a few inches, as if someone   50 was pulling on the rope; then he was dropped quickly and painfully. The nylon cord tugged around his waist. Beck assumed this was Iggy's idea of a joke, and decided to fire him when he got back to the surface. Once more Beck was raised slightly, then with a jolt he fell again. The force of the second drop was enough to snap the cord, and, with no further connections to the earth, Beck began to tumble dizzily into the vortex.

The light overhead faded like the smoke of an ascending rocket. The sides of the Big Hole widened until they were no longer visible; there was only Beck, the flashlight, the broken train of his nylon   60 cord overhead, and the omnipresence of gravity. Beck saw small glowing lights on either side again; there were people in the dollhouses. He saw a small kitchen, a kitchen with people drinking at a table, with a single light bulb hanging down overhead. He recognized himself—but the woman he was drinking with, what was her name? It had all been so long ago, but he remembered that night now, the night the two of them had finished the Old Crow. They would always be friends. What was her name? Woozy? Toozy? Kay-Kay?

There was the machine he had built out of the box the refriger-   70 ator came in. He filled it with light bulbs and punched holes in the sides, then he had crawled into the box and waited for people to put small slips of paper in the slot he had marked ANSWERS TO YOUR

QUESTIONS. Because no one was home, he stayed in the machine all day with the three-by-five cards he had prepared, marked: YES / NO / ALL OF THE ABOVE / NONE OF THE ABOVE. It had been a long time ago, but he had not forgotten.

"I get it," Beck said. "It's an intelligence test." He rolled his eyes. "Everything I can remember grows to life-size. If I remember everything, the hole fills up. If I don't, I fall forever. Damn. What   80 was the name of that woman again? Ariel? Pristrina? Hildegarde?"

His wife and he had gone to the Fulton Street Fishmarket on their first date. The fishmongers had attempted to make them sick by pretending to cut the head off of a turtle with a paring knife. Afterward the two of them had smoked cigars and waltzed on the Brooklyn Bridge. The sound of tires on the bridge below them sounded like a squadron of airplanes. He had loved his wife that night, had known he would marry her. She gave up her teaching job and gave him a son. The fishmonger grew life-size and fell toward him.   90

Everything he had ever forgotten in his life said hello. There was the night he had gone on a date to see *La Traviata;* there were the matches he had borrowed from Inke, who worked at the International Swedish Foundation; there were the martinis they had sipped at the Carlyle. Then Inke had found the two of them together. He had forgotten to read the message she had left for him inside the matchbook. There had been a scene that concluded with the intersection of Beck's haircut and the music stand of the coronet player in the Carlyle house band. Melanie hadn't wanted to see him after that.   100

On the surface, people stood around the Big Hole for some time. After a while people got bored, though, and began to remember the things they had forgone in order to watch the backhoe. There were clocks to set back, for daylight-savings time was ending; there were library books to return, for a grace period had been declared on bad debts. Iggy drained the swimming pool. Verdi got fired from the Egyptian Embassy for singing, and showed up at Beck's house, expressing a great desire to see his old friend. Expecting him back any day, Verdi stayed on, fell in love with Beck's wife, became the scoutmaster of small Beck's cub pack. Eventually the Big Hole 110 disappeared, but this was not noticed because by this time it was forgotten that it had ever existed. The cub scouts planted sunflowers

and corn there. When the corn died, Verdi showed his son how to
gather the dried stalks together and make a scarecrow. They used a
lot of old clothes Verdi could not remember ever having worn. There
was something about the scarecrow that frightened people. So they
dissected it.

56. This is a story about:
   A) The forgetfulness of lovers
   B) The selectivity of the imaginative memory
   C) The nonexistence of elves
   D) The recapitulation of oddness

57. Which of the following is the *worst* opening line for this story:
   A) "My mother died of the laughing disease on the day that President
       Kennedy was assassinated, and for the next few weeks I suffered
       from the delusion that the American people were in mourning
       for her."
   B) "On the morning of the third day a bullet fired by Union troops
       passed through the side of a farmhouse, went through two
       wooden walls and one stone one, and came to rest in the left lung
       of Mrs. Jonathan A. DeWees."
   C) "The summer after his illness Mike was sent to work on his Uncle
       Mort's farm."
   D) "The sun shines down on a rhinestone capsule sparkling on an
       onyx-and-platinum launch pad surrounded by the burgundy-
       colored velvet-and-satin gantry."

58. The best title for this story would be:
   A) "The Hole in the Morning"
   B) "36 Miracles of Millard Fillmore"
   C) "Final Exam"
   D) "Elvis in Space"

59. "Dizzy" in line 57 is an antonym for:
   A) Vertiginous
   B) Giddy
   C) Gillespie
   D) Aunty Em

60. If you were the author of this story, the single worst way of revising
    your work might be:

A) Putting Verdi in the Big Hole instead of Beck

B) Having the story take place among spoiled college kids in New York who have no real problems except taking too many drugs and dancing

C) Eating a lot of "Meow Mix" and drinking barbecue fluid and then crossing off everything that got on your nerves

D) Changing Beck's wife's name to "Goofy"

IN THE FOLLOWING QUESTIONS, COMPLETE THE SENTENCE WITH ONE OF THE WORDS OR PHRASES SUPPLIED:

61. If Beck weren't so ——, he wouldn't have all these ——.
    A) Pretentious : problems
    B) Forgetful : wives
    C) Human : elves
    D) Egyptian : songs

62. The Big Hole can be seen as a(n) —— for ——.
    A) Allegory : laughs
    B) Problem : Iggy
    C) Big Hole : its own sake
    D) Object lesson : spiritual amnesia

63. The —— the ——.
    A) "Egotistical Sublime" of Keats : "Gyres" of Yeats
    B) More you think about this story : dumber it gets
    C) Bigger they come : harder they fall
    D) Closer Beck gets to the center of the earth : more he wishes he had memorized the poetry of Charles Bukowski

64. Beck's —— is a(n) —— to the stomach of Melanie Brown.
    A) Wife : irritation
    B) Trouble : picnic compared
    C) Big Hole : thing very similar
    D) Memory : soothing pink-colored lining

QUESTION 65 (ESSAY)

Beck reaches the bottom of the hole and finds, strewn on the floor, a pair of earplugs, an ashtray bearing the symbol of a budding orchid, a matchbook bearing the initials I.S.F., the sheet music for *La*

Traviata, a faded train ticket, the shell of a small turtle, an olive soaked with what was determined to be three parts gin, one part vermouth, and the masticated remains of schoolroom blackboard chalk. Saint Peter approaches him and puts out his hand.

"Shake?" he says.

Beck shakes.

"So," Saint Peter says. "What did you think?"

"Beats me," Beck says. "You're so smart, why are you dead?"

65. Answer Beck's question in fictional form, using one of the following titles. Your story should have something to do with space flight and must contain at least one celebrity.

A) "Elvis in Space"

B) "Remind Me to Murder You Later"

C) "Robot Girls from Planet Utah"

D) "Invisible Woman"

"Welcome," Peter says. "By the way, there's a woman here who wants to talk to you, and boy is she mad. Third suicide on the left. The one with the ink."

STOP. IF YOU FINISH BEFORE TIME IS
CALLED, YOU MAY REVIEW YOUR WORK.
PLEASE DO NOT GO ON TO OTHER STORIES.

✦ The Rescue

The summer after his illness Mike was sent to work on his Uncle Mort's farm. His father said the country would do him good, give him a chance to think things over. Anyway, Mike's cousin Fred, whom he had never met, had also recently endured an illness. His breath had slowed down to almost nothing, the same as Mike's. It was as if the boys had something in common.

Now, on a morning in October, Mike stares at the ceiling, listening to the birds arise. He should be up by now but he can't bring himself to do it. It's cold outside, but that's not the problem. The problem is Fred. An endless wasting coma would be better than a waking world that contains Fred. The boys do not see eye-to-eye.

Mike grinds his teeth and mutters to himself. He's got to do it. He sits up, swings his feet onto the cold floor. Last night there were rats there. He heard them. They won't get into your bed usually. It would have been better if they were mice, but the only mice on the farm are Fred's supposedly tame ones. Two weeks ago Mike put on his shoes one morning and found Fred's mice in them. Fred laughs like this: huh-*huh* huh-*huh* huh-*huh*.

Mike washes his face with cold water from the spigot marked "hot," puts on yesterday's pants, two plaid shirts, laces up his boots. As he opens the door, tenderly, tenuously, he looks upward to make sure Fred hasn't put a bucket of unpasteurized milk on the transom. He hasn't, at least not yet. The day is cold and clear, and Mike's breath vaporizes in the air.

The lights in the barn are on, which is suspicious. Either he left them on last night, which he doesn't remember doing, or Fred has gotten up extra early to lay a trap for him. Of course, Fred also might have gotten up, turned on the lights, then gone back to bed without setting a trap so that Mike will stand around in the cold wondering what the trap is. It's the kind of thing Fred would do.

As a Quaker, Mike has been taught to ignore people like Fred. The worst punishment for bad people is them having to live their lives. "Evil is its own reward." Just once though, Mike would like to do something evil in return. Not punch Fred, obviously; violence is out. But beat him by making Fred behold his own atrociousness. "I will never cheat thee, but I may outsmart thee." Just once. That's not asking much.

In the barn Watson lows impatiently, bag bursting. Mike doesn't know how to proceed. He creeps forward, looking for signs of trouble. There is no Fred. Watson looks at him, cow breath steaming out of her nostrils.

Mike sits down on the milking stool. Puts the pail beneath Watson's bulging bag. Mike squeezes an udder and gets nothing. "It'll be good for you," Mike's father had said. "You been inside long enough. We need to get you out in the country. Give you a chance to figure out what you want your life to be like."

Five months later, Mike still has trouble making a fist. The muscles in his forearms are weak. If he could make a fist he would be able to milk Watson and then maybe also he would punch Fred. Last night Mike found the legs of his striped pajama bottoms tied into knots. His mother gave him those pajamas. Fred should know there's a line you don't cross. But he doesn't. All Fred knows about is how to make things awful.

A hoof narrowly misses Mike's face. "Goddammit to hell," Mike says. He yanks on a teat and Watson squirts into the pail. Mike's life disgusts him. Each squirt in the pail conjures another image of his own humiliation. *Squoosh.* Mike misses almost all of sixth grade. *Squish.* Mike finds a garter snake in his bed. *Squash.* Mike runs over a yellowjacket nest with the Rototiller. Fred laughs like this: huh-*huh* huh-*huh* huh-*huh*.

Maybe he could somehow run Fred out of breath. Fred's lungs aren't too good, and when he gets all worked up sometimes he has to breathe into one of those oxygen masks. Maybe if he did something that would force Fred to run around, turn blue. Mike isn't the kind of person who likes to be made a fool of. Fred has to learn that.

Uncle Mort was angry but unsurprised when Mike said that today was going to be his last day. He was like a prison warden who has learned one of the inmates has been pardoned by the governor—that is, a lot less gracious than you'd expect. He and Dad probably had a long talk about it. Just once Mike wishes Dad would stand up for him. They probably hadn't even mentioned Fred at all, and Fred was the most important thing.

Mike reaches for the Bag Balm. Watson has an infection on the lower bag which is making her udders too dry and chapped. The Big Balm is kept in a canister above the pails. Mike pops the top off the can and digs his fingers into something that, whatever it is, is definitely *not* Bag Balm.

A half-hour later, Mike is still running freezing water from the tap onto his hand. This doesn't quite do the trick, but what else can he do? Whatever Fred put in the tin was at least partly oil-based. It's the premeditation of it all that gets to Mike. That's the thing. In order to pull this little stunt, Fred had to: a) devise a solution that would burn off a layer of Mike's skin, b) scrape the Bag Balm out of the canister, c) replace it with this burning whatever-it-is, and d) get up early enough in the morning to do all this without running into Mike. Doesn't Fred have anything else to do other than torture someone who has been raised not to fight back?

Uncle Mort pokes his head into the barn. He looks a little like an orang-utan. "What in hell you doing, boy?"

"Milking, sir."

"I thought you said you quit."

"I did."

"Well, if you're all fired up to work on your last day you can get going in the field. We got the frost in last night and everything's dying in the ground."

"I have to find Fred first."

Uncle Mort looks sad, surprised. "I don't want to hear that," he says.

"I'm sorry, Uncle Mort."

"You help me outside then. Come on, git."

Mike is powerless. He follows his uncle out to the beet field. The boys are Uncle Mort's only help on the farm. He used to have a hand called The Swede but he got the same breathing disease that Fred had. He was a giant of a man, short on words, and did little besides working and eating except for occasionally tooting on a special harmonica. Without the Swede, Uncle Mort is bent over in the field alone, pulling beets out of the ground and throwing them into a basket.

"Get going," Uncle Mort says.

Mike collapses on his knees in the cold earth. For acres and acres around him there are beets, frozen and dying in the earth. Mike pulls a frozen beet out of the ground, then feels a shadow upon him. Fred's dog, Hooty, is approaching, slowly growling at Mike and showing his teeth.

"Uncle Mort," Mike yells. "Can you please call off your dog?"

"He was Fred's dog," Uncle Mort says.

"Well, can you call Fred's dog off then, please, sir?"

"I don't have any influence with that dog. You know that."

Mike wishes he had told his father to pick him up sooner. He gives the dog a beet. Do dogs like beets? Hooty draws near, saliva slathering from his greenish teeth, a repulsive canine odor drifting forward into the cold. The dog starts to make an awful sound like a loose, liquid choking. Aglugh, aglugh, aglugh. Hooty's stomach is contracting, and his eyes are growing large. Aglugh, aglugh, aglugh. There is an eruption of dog liquid, which runs like lava onto the frozen beet field. Mike thinks, I guess they don't.

Hooty looks at what he has done, then looks at Mike. He begins to growl and takes a step forward.

Suddenly a beet bounces off of the dog's skull. Hooty looks like he has just remembered his lost puppyhood. With a glazed expression, he wanders away.

Mike ducks. A beet passes over his head. If he could trace the trajectory of the beet to its launch pad, he would know the exact position of Fred. Suddenly a clod of earth hits Mike in the forehead. Uncle Mort stands looking at his nephew, turning red.

"That's what you get for wasting food!" Uncle Mort says. "Now you pick until that beet is paid for!"

"But Uncle Mort," Mike says. "Fred threw it. Not me."

Uncle Mort looks pained. "What's wrong with you?" he says. "Why do you have to say that? You don't think that hurts to hear you say that? What's wrong with you, you got no sense?"

"I've got sense."

Mike hears Fred laughing at him from the hen house, or at least it sounds like laughter for a moment before the laughs are engulfed by coughing. Fred is standing next to a broken tractor, coughing into his fist. Uncle Mort looks away.

"I'm sorry," Mike says.

"You ain't sorry," Uncle Mort says. "You never knew him. What do you have to be sorry about?"

"But I am," Mike says. "I still am."

At quarter to twelve, the rain begins to fall onto the frozen field. After a few moments it turns to hail, and the hailstones bounce and roll down the piles of frozen beets. Uncle Mort remains doubled over, hail bouncing off his back. Mike stands in the rain and feels drowsy. He looks toward the shack where his things are and leaves the field.

"Where you going, boy?" Uncle Mort calls after him, but Mike does not hear him. He goes back to the shack and falls into bed, moist. Four hours still before his father rescues him.

The day outside gets darker and darker, and the rain and hail on the roof sound like a snare drum. The light seems to waver a little bit. Mike has noticed this: sometimes the air is a little thin on the farm, as if there is gas in it. On public television one time they explained about Venus. The surface of Venus is a continuous thunderstorm of liquid methane. It's supposed to be as much like hell as anyplace in the solar system. Sometimes Uncle Mort's farm is like this, too.

Mike reaches underneath his bed and gets out the suitcase he brought with him five months ago. He opens the beat-up drawer of the old wardrobe and dumps his shirts and jeans in. He opens the other drawer, where his underwear is. He looks twice. There is a spider on top of his underwear. A big spider. Mike knows that tarantulas are a lot faster than you think. They can move at something like a hundred miles an hour when they're mad.

"Goddammit to hell," Mike says. The tarantula starts to move.

Mike leaves the shack, quickly, and goes around to the front of his Uncle's house. There is the smell of apples cooking in the kitchen. Two apple pies are cooling on a windowsill, next to a large bowl of applesauce. Aunt Mary makes it special. Mike opens the refrigerator and finds a liverwurst sandwich inside of waxed paper marked "Mike." This is also my last day for liverwurst, he thinks, biting into the pumpernickel. Mike opens a quart of milk and guzzles it straight from the carton.

In the "remedy drawer," next to the Tylenol and the Bufferin and the Ipecac Syrup, is a half-empty bottle of Ex-Lax pills. Mike is thinking. He dumps the Ex-Lax into a small cereal bowl. With the back of a spoon, Mike crushes the pills into a fine powder, then dumps it into Fred's applesauce. With three rotations of the spoon, the task is completed. He smiles guiltily and walks back out through the rain to the shack. The tarantula is gone.

In an hour Uncle Mort and Aunt Mary are inside, eating lunch. While everyone's in the kitchen, Mike goes out to the toolshed. He has an idea. He finds the acetylene torch and the tinderbox and sneaks toward the outhouse. There is a half-moon upon the door.

Mike stands in the outhouse. This idea doesn't seem so good now. Outside, the rain is coming down hard. Someone's feet are squashing through the mud. It's do or die. Mike takes a deep breath, hopes for the best, and lowers himself through the outhouse hole, into the dark. Now he's down there. It's not as bad as you might think. You get used to it. There is another Quaker saying, "Those that know how can live comfortably even in hell."

The seat, eight feet overhead, throws a dim spotlight into the netherworld. You can learn a lot about people this way. The light is strange, though, thin, like it got on the farm sometimes, as if the gas was coming in again. He opens up the valve on the torch and scrapes the tinder. A small blue flame appears.

Mike turns the torch up high and hears a funny sound, almost like a distant music. It's like there is a violin or something. Fred's face appears in the hole overhead, like the face of God surrounded by all the light in the universe.

"Hey Mike," Fred says. "What are you doing down there?"

Mike smiles. This is his moment. "I'm waiting for you, Fred," Mike says. "You have to admit I got you this time."

Fred smiles too. "Yup," he says. "You got me all right. I got to hand it to you."

He honks a little bit on a harmonica. "You like that, Mike? I stole it from The Swede. I told him I'd seen you with it last."

Mike looks at Fred as if he is trying to see a distant planet in the sky. Fred coughs into his fist, and pauses. Mike can hear his heavy asthmatic breathing.

"By the way, Fred," Mike says, "how was your applesauce?"

"Oh that," Fred says. "I didn't eat that. I knew you'd put the rest of the Ex-Lax in it."

"The rest of the what?"

"The first half of the bottle was in your sandwich," Fred says. "In the liverwurst. But I guess you know that."

"Sure," Mike says.

"You want to know what I did with the applesauce?" Fred says.

"Uh-huh."

"I gave it to ol'Hooty."

"Oh."

"Want to know where he is?"

"Sure."

"He's down there with you."

Mike squints into the corner. Hooty walks over damp, dark mountains toward him.

"I know you guys have problems," Fred says. "Maybe now you two can be friends. He's really a good dog."

Fred's face suddenly contorts with surprise. There is a soft scream, then Fred plummets head first through the hole. He lands on top of Hooty. There is nothing but light for a moment, then a square face appears overhead.

"I told you a tousand tousand times," The Swede says to Fred, "don't mess mit my harmonicas."

The Swede disappears. Light from outside rises and falls as the outhouse door opens and closes. Mike's father will never find him now. Not down here.

Hooty bites Fred in the leg, then wags his tail. There is that music again, louder now. There is a glow of purple in a soft plain beyond the hills. "What is that?" Mike says, looking at his cousin.

Fred and Hooty are standing now, looking down a narrow road that vanishes in fog. "Hey Fred," he says. "Can you tell me what that is?"

"Paradise," says his cousin.

✦ Elvis in Space

The sun shines down on a rhinestone capsule sparkling on an onyx-and-platinum launch pad surrounded by the burgundy-colored velvet-and-satin gantry. We can't quite see him but we know he's in there. Everybody knows about it. The liquid oxygen in mother-of-pearl inlaid compression tanks, the cork-lined throttle controls imported from France, the helmet made of Waterford crystal: there's been nothing else in the news for weeks.

Countdown stands at less than three minutes and counting. A problem with trajectory monitoring seems to have been remedied, and we are now go for launch. Journalists from around the world are speaking—Japanese, German, French, Yugoslavian, Russian—into microphones. Something big is definitely happening here. We're all wearing NASA patches embroidered with Elvis's initials and a small silhouette of a Les Paul guitar levitating above an idealized portrait of earthrise as seen from the Sea of Fertility which is lavender.

There is a slight disturbance from the bleachers now as we stand at slightly more than two and a half minutes to go. Someone claiming to have seen Elvis actually waving from the capsule has started a sudden rush of spectators trying to see him. Of course, it's not possible that anyone has actually seen Elvis—he's been strapped into his Louis XIV launch couch for well over four hours now—but people have been staring through binoculars for so long that anything is possible. There is a slight chance that Elvis did undo the restraining belts and move toward the window to wave, but we cannot be certain of that at this time. It seems like a somewhat dangerous move for him to make, in clear violation of his flight commands. The danger for Elvis is that he might not be able to get back into position before launch time. That would make the next hour or so extremely uncomfortable for him. He'd bounce around.

We haven't heard any sound from the capsule since Elvis indicated that he was feeling "good" an hour ago. Elvis suggested, prior to boarding the capsule, that he did not intend to keep a running commentary going. "I don't think that's dignified," he said. If Elvis did get up, however, it's more likely he went looking for his guitar than waving from the window, since that kind of waving motion has got to be difficult in the capsule's cramped quarters. Also, Elvis is on his back, so even if he did get his hand over to the window to wave, he probably couldn't fit his face there, too.

Earlier, I spoke with Duke Meyerhoff, commander of two Gemini missions and scheduled captain of *Apollo 19*, the April 1974 voyage to the moon that was canceled when Congress cut back on NASA funding. Duke, do you think it's possible that Elvis was waving from the capsule, and if so, do you think we can expect to see him wave again before launch time?

"Jim, I'd have to say I don't believe Elvis was waving up there. Your eyes can play tricks on you when you try to look at things far away. Sometimes if you're alone you can even think you see ghosts or something out of one corner of your eye, but, if you look at them, they aren't there really at all."

So you think this waving is just something people are imagining?

"I didn't say that Jim, but it's got to be cramped in the capsule for Elvis, and I'd bet he's a lot more concerned with his prelaunch checklist than he is with waving his glove out the window. On the other hand, he is known for his dedication to his fans. I'd say that of all the people most likely to disregard the checklist in order to wave probably Elvis is up there near the top, but still you have to remember he's got a lot to do right now, a tremendous lot, so I'd say that if there was anyone waving, and I'm not saying there was, but I'm saying if there was though, it was probably a technician. There are a lot of support staff up there and probably one of the people monitoring the liquid oxygen intakes just figured, what the heck, why not give a wave to people. Either that or Elvis got their attention and asked somebody to wave for him."

Elvis's guitar has been sealed in an aluminum vacuum pack and is being basted in a continuous bath of boiled nitrogen in order to keep it in tune. You can see from our animation here that tuning the guitar in space is an extremely dangerous process, and would necessitate an extravehicular activity, EVA, or "space walk," in which Elvis would take the guitar out of the vacuum pack while keeping his back turned from the sun to keep the ultraviolet rays from exerting their corrosive powers on the steel strings. Even though Elvis's guitar strings have been expressly triple-wound in zinc so as to hold up under zero gravity, there is always the chance of one of them being wound too tight and breaking. There are no backup strings.

What sort of danger does this flight offer for Elvis? I asked Duke Meyerhoff.

"The personal risk to Elvis should not be underestimated, Jim, yet we do believe that these risks are within acceptable mission limits. The most immediate risk to Elvis concerns the effect of the tremendous G-forces on his voice. Back in the Gemini launches a couple different astronauts found it hard to carry a tune. On *Gemini 8* in particular, after the capsule failed to rendezvous with the Agena docking probe, we were all pretty quiet. There just wasn't all that—I don't know how to put this, I guess you'd have to say there wasn't much to sing about then. Elvis, of course, might react completely differently."

Do you think there's any personal danger to Elvis? Some commentators have suggested something might go wrong with his brain.

"Jim, there is the possibility he might lose some of his memory; as you know the capsule's going to be heading through the Van Allen radiation belt, and that does have some effect on what we call the Zeta fluid cells— the memory 'building blocks' in the fluid that actually supports the brain inside the skull. You know the G-forces get the Z-cells awfully stirred up, and there is a kind of low-gravity carbonation that can take place inside the mind. The net effect of this is twofold: not only can Elvis get a permanent or temporary loss of memory, but we on Earth might also temporarily or permanently forget about him, depending on the force of the carbonation and also on the way the foam gets blown around, assuming that it does. So in short, Jim, I'd have to say that Elvis is taking a risk here but I'm sure he's aware of the risk he's taking. That's why everyone's so proud and that's why we're all here today in the first place."

With less than thirty seconds to go, we still haven't heard anything from the capsule. We're assuming Elvis is just tongue tied. The silence is eerie, though, you'd have to say, not what you'd expect in front of all these people. Everyone is very quiet now, looking up at the Redstone rocket with the words UNITED STATES painted onto the side and the big picture of Elvis underneath it with the sun rising behind him which is magenta.

A small cloud of white smoke is moving from the liquid fuel tanks now. There's no movement visible in the windows of the capsule. If Elvis was waving before, he's not waving now. Or if he is, we can't see it.

Seven seconds and ignition sequence start. The earth begins to rumble below us. Smoke and fire engulf the base of the rocket; Elvis's picture is half-buried in white clouds. We have lift-off, repeat, we have lift-off. At quarter past the hour. We have cleared the tower. There is applause here on the ground. People are crying and hugging. The mood in mission control could be called exuberant. The men are shaking hands over their monitors at the Johnson Space Center in Houston, and people are opening champagne bottles and playing old 45 records and dancing the way they used to do. It's a beautiful bird, a beautiful thing to watch. Go, baby, go.

As the first stage separates from the second, we haven't yet heard any confirmation from the capcom as to Elvis's condition. We assume he's inside and doing fine. Everything is going according to the book, mission-wise. The launch occurred exactly on schedule, leaving a wide berth here in the launch envelope. We're still awaiting word from the ground as to how Elvis is doing.

The smoke is clearing from the pad, drifting toward the spectators. We can smell the sulfur and the ozone as the vapor drifts past. People are taking photographs of the smoke, putting their binoculars away. We can see lots of happy faces, folks heading back toward their cars. The hot dog vendors are putting their umbrellas down. The rocket is only a tiny dot now, like a star in a blue sky. If you lose track of it for a moment you can't find it again. It's little.

Elvis is approaching the Van Allen radiation belt. It must be getting very hot inside the capsule. We can only hope things are going well. There is some suggestion that there has been a sort of breakdown in capsule communications. We think there's something wrong with his microphone. If the microphone was working, we're sure Elvis would be talking, describing the good earth. He would be describing the view of our living planet out there in all that blackness and red heat of the radiation belt now, because it is all supposed to be very beautiful.

Many of the cars and buses are crowding onto the highway, but traffic is slow because a lot of people are looking up at the sky while they're driving. Many of the spectators are listening to the news on their car radios. You can't get away from it. It's on every channel. They're broadcasting the static from the capsule. It sounds like a 45, crackling beneath the needle of an old-fashioned record player.

Wait a minute. Something is happening. Something is definitely happening. We have a report that the zeta fluid has bubbles in it. Big ones. Something's gotten carbonated. There's fizzing.

And now he's singing. Or somebody is. "Where the blue of the night," he's crooning, "meets the gold of the day . . . " He's talking about

Minute Maid orange juice. There is an unconfirmed report of golf clubs floating around the capsule. The president is calling Bob Hope. "Love me tender," he's singing, but the voice is way too low. "Love me true." We are continuing to monitor the situation. "Never let me go." Einstein was right.

✦ Pickett's Charge

for Tim Kreider

On the morning of the third day a bullet fired by Union troops passed through the side of a farmhouse, went through two wooden walls and a stone one, and came to rest in the left lung of Mrs. Jonathan A. DeWees. General Lewis Addison Armistead looked down at his men from the saddle of his horse and said, "Who will follow me?" The soldiers began to march across the burning Pennsylvania cornfield, as bands played the songs of attack. Armistead drew his sword. "Let's give'em cold steel, boys!" he said.

Burvil, Jonah, and Jennifer sat by the wall that protected the front line of the Union army, eating chili cheese dogs and lime slushies. "I heard during the fighting here there was one guy who was so scared he bayoneted his own head," Burvil said.

"Shut up," Jennifer said, "You're gross." She turned down the volume of her lavender plastic cassette player.

"Yeah, bayoneted his own head and everything."

"That's not possible," Jonah said nervously, thinking about it.

"Bayoneted his own brain."

Jennifer sucked on her slushie, looking across the undulating field toward the distant line of green trees. The field was divided in half by a small road, next to which ran a long unpainted fence. A girl wearing blue shorts and a white polo shirt was walking across the battlefield toward the Confederate side.

"What's wrong with Erica?" Jonah said.

"Who cares," said Jennifer. "She is like a total geek."

The shelling had gone on for hours. Suddenly, there was silence from the Union barricades. The order to march was given. The only thing that stood between the Confederates and the Union troops was the fence that ran next to the Mechanicsburg road. The generals assured the men that it would yield before the pressure of so many.

Erica sat down on the fence. Behind her, up the short rise of the field, were her classmates, eating their lunches. Mr. Davis and Ms. Midgely-Biggs were standing by the monument to General Armistead called *The High Water Mark of the Confederacy*. It marked the point at which

Armistead fell, the furthest penetration of Union lines by a member of the Confederate army.

This was what it was like, Erica thought. She had always thought it would be more dramatic, that she would have something to say. But there were no words. Just the feeling that there was another world somewhere, a world in which the invisible was more familiar.

Mr. Davis looked up at her, sitting by herself on the fence, then said something to Ms. Midgely-Biggs. Probably talking about me. Midgely-Biggs is a bitch and a half; when she gets excited, she stutters and looks upward into her own brain, so all you can see from the outside is the white part, like two peeled hard-boiled eggs. Midgely-Biggs was part of the problem, the reason why she was sure there was another world. And people like her. It was the putridness of this world that suggested to Erica that a better one was possible.

In the farmhouse to the south, Mrs. DeWees made bread. The battle—which had started by accident, which was not even supposed to be taking place here at all—had been going on for two days. The ranks of the Confederate charge were splitting in half in order to go around the DeWees house and barn. In about an hour, the Forty-eighth Regiment of the Army of Vermont will wipe out the smaller flank, then do an about-face and begin to attack the larger flank, headed by Armistead. Mrs. DeWees carefully removes the brown loaves from the oven and places them on the window to cool.

"Oh no," Burvil said, "Look who's coming."

"Oh, God," Jennifer said. "It's Tony Mendicino."

"What does he want?" Jonah said.

"God knows," Burvil said. "But here he comes."

"Huh huh huh huh hi guys," Tony said. He held his hand in front of his mouth because spit sliding off his lips and braces sprayed the general area in front of him as he spoke. His fingers and hands twitched in spasms as he attempted to force himself over parts of sentences his stutter refused to let him negotiate. "I wuh wuh wuh wuh I wuh I wuh was wuh wondering if yuh yuh you had seen my puh my puh had seen my puh pocketnuhknife."

"No, we haven't seen your puh pocketnuhknife," said Burvil. "Did you lose it?"

"Yuh yuh yuh yuh—you're sure you duh don't huh have it?"

"What do we want with your stupid knife?"

"Yeah, what do we want with it?"

"It was my fah fah fah it was my fah my father's."

"Gee whiz, Tony, say it, don't spray it, okay?"

The fence adjoining the Mechanicsburg road did not yield. The posts had been driven too deeply into the earth. The Confederate forces had to break ranks and climb over the wall, then reform columns on the other side. For twenty minutes the Union forces watched them grow nearer and nearer, marching in long gray files. General Meade instructed his men to practice the presentation of arms, just as in training camp, in order to keep them from watching the advancing Confederate charge. Smoke hung heavy in the air. The music of victorious Confederate bands was everywhere.

I am never going to say anything again in my life, Tony Mendicino thought. Not until my braces are off and I stop stuttering and everything is different. They think they're so smart, sitting there and laughing. Well, I can be smart, too, and if I don't say anything, but just look at them with my special eyes, people will know I'm smart but they won't know exactly why because I won't say what I'm thinking. Eventually people will forget my name and they will only call me The Silent One. Everyone will fear the eye of The Silent One, especially the ones that laughed before he gave up talking.

There is no accurate record of where Pickett was during the charge that bears his name. By some accounts he remained back behind the lines, near Lee's headquarters. There are accounts that he spent much of the time brushing his long brown hair and putting on cologne. Other stories have him closer to the front, just south of the DeWees farmhouse. We know that he survived the massacre and returned that evening to General Lee, who said, "Pickett, order your division to follow me to Cemetery Ridge." Pickett looked back at Lee and said, "General, I have no division."

Erica walked down the field toward the farmhouse. The ground rose and fell; the grass was yellow, flecked with a little green. The day was bright, the sky pale blue. One hundred twenty-four years ago it was ninety-six degrees. The soldiers' uniforms were woolen. Their blood ran into this ground, still feeds the grass probably. There's something about this place. It's all grown over but you can still tell it's been torn up underneath.

The barn next to the DeWees house was filled with bales of hay. There were no animals. A hole remained in the loft wall below the hex sign where a cannonball went through July 3, 1863. It's quiet. The only sound is some crickets, chirping in this bright July haze. It's cool inside the barn, though, and it feels good to lie down in the hay, to cover yourself with the thin stalks. Erica pulled out the knife and looked at its long, cool edge.

Mr. Davis had been giving them essays almost every day. Some of them you could fake, like "My Earliest Memory." Tony Mendicino had the weirdest memory, something about *Apollo 13,* the one that almost blew up in space. Tony acts like he knows something but he won't say what it is. Maybe what he knows is that thing he has to say cannot be spoken. Still, he might drop hints sometimes. Maybe send out semaphore.

Mr. Davis had rejected Erica's essay "My Greatest Fear." No one is that afraid of ticks, he said. So she went back to the study hall and wrote "Afraid to Care," about growing up with only brothers and wanting to be a boy and playing football with them and going hiking. Then when her father died, she hadn't cried, only left the room and walked around and hung out with her brothers' friends at the public swimming pool and went skin diving for Band-aids. So she wrote an essay about all of this and Mr. Davis, whom the kids secretly call Shaggy because of his resemblance to a cartoon character on the "Scooby-Doo" show, has fallen over himself praising her "candor and honesty" and has nominated her for the Newfield Award, which has something to do with scholarship money that she doesn't want even if she wins, which she won't.

The Union troops open fire all at once. Armistead realizes he has walked into a trap. The northern troops only pretended to be out of ammunition to draw them in. Now the jaws of the trap close around them, and, one after the other, the Confederate soldiers fall. They have to march right over the corpses in order not to break formation. Some of them, like Armistead, get as far as the stone wall at the top of the field, and then there is hand-to-hand fighting, with bayonets and fists and rocks. Armistead's horse is shot out from under him and he falls, mortally wounded, twenty feet from something called the Clump of Trees.

Erica was not sure what the other world was like. She didn't think it had to be all that different from this one. Just a few minor changes. The social setup. And the feelings that you had there didn't sweep you around as much. Things had a better feel over there. They let you get a grip. And the things that you counted on didn't disappear.

She held the knife in one hand. With the other she unbuttoned one button of her shirt, right next to the little horse, and tried to remember which side her heart was on. Her father had a purple birthmark on his chest, which she didn't notice until he got sick. She held the knife against her skin. All I have to do now is push it in. I will disappear in this silent barn if I only push it in.

A figure appeared in the door, a tall gray shadow with a menacing profile. He looked around the barn, then stared right at her. She could see what she thought were teeth, gleaming. He put out a long, skeletal hand, summoning her to him, commanding her to rise.

Erica pretended she could not see him, but no one can disobey the summons of The Silent One. She stood up and went to him. Still saying nothing, he reached out his hand. There was something fierce about his eyes. Something from the other world. He took the knife from her, looked at it as if it were his own, put it in his pocket. Then she gave him her hand. They stood in the hay together, then moved forward in silence.

The bullet, passing through an outer wall and two inner ones, came to rest in the lungs of Mrs. DeWees. She fell to the floor, her bread still cooling on the windowsill. Outside, the fighting went on. A cannonball sailed over the house, arced above the chimney, pounded through the wall of the barn, leaving a hole almost perfectly round, slightly flattened out on one side, like a summer moon just past full.

Erica and Tony Mendicino, smiling, courageous, ran in a slow diagonal across the undulating hill, toward the Union barricades, where Burvil and Jonah and Jennifer and the rest of the class were listening to rock-'n'-roll and finishing their lunches. "Let's give'em cold steel, boys," Erica said. Their adversaries, uncertain, stood waiting by the Clump of Trees, eyeing them nervously from the other side of a long stone wall.

Designed by Martha Farlow
Composed by Blue Heron in Plantin
Printed by R. R. Donnelley and Sons Company on 55-lb. Cream White Sebago
and bound in Holliston Aqualite on spine and Kingston Natural on sides